"When Did You Find Out?"

Matt asked.

"Right before I met you. That's why I didn't want to get involved." She reached up and caressed his cheek. "I tried to fight loving you. I really did."

Matt grinned ruefully. "So I recall. But that's all over now. No more pretending. No more secrets." He took her hands in his and promised solemnly, "We'll get through this together, Meg."

"But, Matt," she protested. "It's not your problem. I have to deal with this alone."

He cupped her chin in his hands and gazed into her eyes. There Meg saw more love than any woman had a right to hope for. "Don't ever let me hear you say that again," he said vehemently. "I love you, Meg Blake, and there's no way I'm walking out on you now."

Dear Reader:

Series and Spin-offs! Connecting characters and intriguing interconnections to make your head whirl.

In Joan Hohl's successful trilogy for Silhouette Desire— *Texas Gold* (7/86), *California Copper* (10/86), *Nevada Silver* (1/87)—Joan created a cast of characters that just wouldn't quit. You figure out how *Lady Ice* (5/87) connects. And in August, "J.B." demanded his own story—*One Tough Hombre*. In *Falcon's Flight*, coming in November, you'll learn *all* about . . .?

Annette Broadrick's *Return to Yesterday* (6/87) introduced Adam St. Clair. This August *Adam's Story* tells about the woman who saves his life—and teaches him a thing or two about love!

The six Branigan brothers appeared in Leslie Davis Guccione's *Bittersweet Harvest* (10/86) and *Still Waters* (5/87). September brings *Something in Common*, where the eldest of the strapping Irishmen finds love in unexpected places.

Midnight Rambler by Linda Barlow is in October—a special Halloween surprise, and totally unconnected to anything.

Keep an eye out for other Silhouette Desire favorites— Diana Palmer, Dixie Browning, Ann Major and Elizabeth Lowell, to name a few. You never know when secondary characters will insist on their own story. . . .

All the best,

Isabel Swift
Senior Editor & Editorial Coordinator
Silhouette Books

SHERRYL WOODS
A Gift of Love

Silhouette Desire

Published by Silhouette Books New York

America's Publisher of Contemporary Romance

SILHOUETTE BOOKS
300 East 42nd St., New York, N.Y. 10017

Copyright © 1987 by Sherryl Woods

ISBN: 0-373-05375-4

First Silhouette Books printing September 1987

America's Publisher of Contemporary Romance

Printed in the U.S.A.

SHERRYL WOODS

lives by the ocean, which provides daily inspiration for the romance in her soul. Her years as a television critic taught her about steamy plots and humor. Her years as a travel editor took her to exotic locations. Her years as a crummy, weekend tennis player taught her to stick with what she enjoyed most: writing. What better way to combine all of that than by writing romantic stories about wonderful heroines, sensitive heroes and enchanting locations.

One

___

Amber liquid swirled in Matt Flanagan's glass. As he sat hunched over the bar, he could remember every word of this afternoon's conversation with Duncan Blake. There had been few of them. The cryptic meeting had offered less illumination than a minimally worded telegram.

The minute he'd entered Duncan's study in his stately home located in the rolling Virginia hills outside Washington, he'd known there was something different about the old man. For the first time in the fifteen years Matt had known him, Duncan looked his age and the retired general had to be at least seventy. To Matt's dismay, Duncan's normally ramrod-straight shoulders were stooped, and the spirit that usually lit his eyes had vanished, leaving them a faded blue. They reminded Matt of jeans that had been washed too many times, seen too much wear.

Lord knew, at his age and with his history of dedicated military service, Duncan had a right to look exhausted once in a while. However, Matt had never seen him that way. He'd never known that the tough old bird could be vulnerable. The realization had shaken him.

Duncan's astonishing request had disturbed him even more. He'd given him a photograph, a small snapshot lovingly framed in sterling silver, then pleaded simply, "Find her for me, Matt."

Matt had gazed at the face in the picture and felt as though something was torn loose inside him. A knife blade held against his throat would have been more familiar than the odd, unexpected sensation that seemed to hold his heart in its grip. Blue eyes, as brilliant as the old man's had once been, filled with excitement and life, had stared back at him. Chestnut hair fell in shining waves around a delicate face that could have been on the cover of any magazine. Full lips, barely tinted pink, tilted crookedly in an infectious grin. The only flaw—and to Matt it was an endearing one—was a tiny chip in a front tooth, making that sunny smile even more delightful.

On closer inspection, he decided the girl couldn't be more than sixteen or seventeen, which made his thoroughly male reaction to her all the more astonishing. At thirty-five, Matt did not seem to be going through the same midlife crisis as some of his friends, a crisis that seemed to draw them to younger women. Matt had nothing to prove and he preferred his women to be his equal in every way. Relationships worked best when the partners shared similar values and perspectives on life. It also helped if they'd had similar experiences, if they too could recall when the Beatles had performed on *Ed Sullivan* or when the Everly Brothers had been together the first time. This gorgeous, innocent child was unlikely to remember any of that.

"Who is she?" he'd asked Duncan, unaware of the breathlessness that made his voice a choked whisper.

"Her name's Margaret, though I think she's calling herself Meg these days. Meg Blake."

Even with all his experience at hiding his reactions, Matt's gold-flecked green eyes had widened perceptibly. "She's your..." His voice had trailed off in confusion. He realized he knew very little about Duncan's personal life with one exception: he had a son about whom he rarely spoke.

"She's my granddaughter. Her daddy's that damned fool son of mine."

The explosive relationship between Duncan and Jonathan Blake was notorious in Washington social circles. The two men had engaged in many public sparring matches in recent years. Now, only an opportunistic hostess hoping to use that feud to gain entry into the society pages dared invite both men to the same occasion. No one knew what had caused the rift between father and son, only that it was enduring and bitter.

"Why do you need me?" Matt had asked.

"You're a detective, aren't you?"

"Yes, but—"

"Matt, the girl's in trouble. I need to find her before it's too late."

"What kind of trouble?"

The old man had shaken his head, then turned away, but not before Matt had seen tears welling up in his eyes. Those tears more than anything had convinced him to do whatever he could for his old mentor.

"Find her, please. That's all I ask," Duncan pleaded. "If my information is right, if she really is in danger, get her to come to me. Tell her I'm here for her, no matter what she thinks."

He turned back, and to Matt's amazement there was the slightest suggestion of a twinkle in his eye as he warned, "Be careful how you tell her, though. She's got my temper and a mind of her own. She won't take kindly to a stranger meddling in her problems."

"Then why send me? Why not go after her yourself?"

"She wouldn't like that one bit, either. It's better that you go. She might listen to you."

"You're talking in circles. What sort of trouble has your granddaughter gotten herself into? Is she flunking out of school?" Matt couldn't help the sarcasm. Although he was more than willing to help his friend's granddaughter if there was real trouble, he didn't have time to waste chasing after some irresponsible kid.

"You don't need to know that," Duncan had said with finality, and Matt knew the tone and the phrase well. He'd heard it often enough during his years in the service. But now that he was in business for himself, running a one-man private investigating firm with an answering machine for a secretary, he wanted more from his clients, even a man he owed as much as Duncan Blake.

"That's not good enough, sir. I want to know what I'm walking into."

"Hell, Flanagan, I'm not sending you into a war zone," the old man had snapped back with some of his former vigor. Matt had winced and only barely refrained from saluting.

He sighed in resignation. "Exactly where are you sending me?"

"You might try some of the bars in Georgetown for starters. I hear she's a regular."

Matt's startled gaze went from Duncan's face to the photo and back again.

"It's an old picture," Duncan said, answering the unspoken question. "Now, get moving, son. If my source is accurate, there's not a minute to lose."

Before what? Matt wondered for the hundredth time as he downed the last of his bourbon and held out his glass for another. What danger could Meg Blake be in that would literally terrify a man who'd led troops into battle without an outward sign of nervousness?

Matt hated operating blind like this. Once before in his life, in a Central American jungle, he'd walked unprepared into a dangerous situation and Duncan Blake had saved his hide. His youthful sureness in tatters, Matt had sworn never to walk into a blind situation again. Now the old man was calling in his debt, sending Matt into the middle of who-knew-what and expecting him to keep his flanks and Meg's covered without knowing a damned thing about where the dangers lurked.

As he tried to think through the possibilities, he kept one eye on the door. It had taken only a few phone calls to old friends at the once-familiar bars around Georgetown to get a fix on where Meg Blake spent her evenings. It had been so simple, Matt continued to be surprised Duncan hadn't made the calls himself.

Finally he'd realized that the General didn't just want Meg found. He wanted her protected and knew he could count on Matt to do just that. Also, for reasons he hadn't chosen to reveal, Duncan knew perfectly well that Meg wouldn't welcome the protection. If she was as headstrong as her granddaddy said, there was no doubt about her viewing it as interference, Matt thought dismally. How the hell was he supposed to baby-sit a grown woman, if she didn't want him around?

Before he could come up with the answer, the door opened and a group of ten or twelve boisterous, expensively attired young people in their twenties burst in. Clearly this was not their first stop of the evening. A couple of the men were cheerfully singing a current pop tune, their voices wildly off-key, and the women had a frenzied, determined gaiety about them.

"Hey, Tony, send over some bottles of your best champagne. We're celebrating," they called to the bartender as they pushed tables together as if they owned the place. Within minutes they had turned the dimly lit bar into their own private party room.

"You're always celebrating," Tony called back, as Matt surveyed them closely, fully expecting to find those clear, laughing blue eyes and full pink lips among them. He glanced at Tony, who shook his head.

"She hangs out with this crowd, but she'd not here yet. She comes in alone and usually leaves alone."

"But you do expect her?"

"Hey, like I told you earlier, the woman's in here every night. Sit tight, Flanagan. She'll show up."

As though the words had been timed by a scriptwriter, the door opened and a woman wrapped in a fur jacket blew in with a gust of icy air.

"Here's your lady now," Tony said.

Matt's eyes started low—on the leather boots so finely made he could imagine the luxurious feel of their buttery softness. Then his gaze traveled slowly and appreciatively up legs that were reed thin in their tight jeans. Next, to the fox jacket that gave an illusion of full curves, but Matt suspected it was just that, an illusion. He hesitated before allowing his gaze to go on, almost afraid of what he would see. The image he recalled from Duncan Blake's photograph had so enchanted him that somehow he couldn't bear the thought of that perfect face being changed.

He took a sip of bourbon, then forced himself to look. The luxuriant hair was the same, waves and waves of brown with intriguing flashes of red cascad-

ing midway down her back. The lips wore a darker
shade of lipstick, but they were just as kissable as he'd
remembered, the bottom lip full and sensual. As her
lips parted on a low, throaty laugh, his breath caught
at the beguiling sight of that chipped front tooth. He
wondered how she'd done it and imagined her falling
from a tree, then getting up laughing, despite scraped
knees and a broken tooth.

Then, when he couldn't stand it another second, his
glance encountered her eyes and it was as if the
warmth that had been growing in him had been
doused by a bucket of ice water. Despite the laughter,
the blue eyes were empty. He'd never seen anyone who
looked more alone in a crowd and impulsively he
wanted to hold her until the impression of sheer joy
he'd imagined in that old photograph was reality. But
this feeling wasn't the reaction of a man who was at-
tracted to a woman, though Meg Blake was one hell of
a beautiful woman. It was the gut-level instinct of one
human being wanting to protect another who was
hurting.

Oddly affected and puzzled by that reaction, Matt
sat at the bar and watched the group for the better part
of an hour, noting the carefree hilarity and teasing in-
teraction among the men and women. Some seemed
paired up but the rest were clearly along just for the
joyride. Meg seemed to be among the latter group.
Although she danced with graceful abandon to the
rock music that blared from giant stereo speakers, she
never danced with the same man twice. Matt suspected she wasn't even aware half the time of which

man was on the floor with her. She danced with her
eyes closed, her head thrown back, her body gyrating
in time to the music, spinning to the edge of control
and back again.

He'd been right about the jacket, he observed as she
twirled within inches of him. She was slender from
head to toe, her figure as fashionably thin as any
model's, though perhaps not so tall. She was no more
than five-foot-six. A height just right for his own five-
foot-ten, he thought as a wave of awareness sped along
his nerves and sent his senses reeling.

She's out of your league, Flanagan, he reminded
himself. Not only that, old man Blake wants you to
protect the woman, not seduce her.

First, though, you've got to meet her.

His opportunity came when she pulled a slim gold
lighter and matching cigarette case from her purse. He
slid off the bar stool and ambled over, wondering exactly how she was likely to react to one of the oldest
gambits in the book. For once he was thankful that he
hadn't stopped carrying cigarettes, even though he'd
given up smoking four months ago. It was like having
a pacifier in his pocket. As long as the pack was there,
he knew he *could* have one. It was a test of his will that
he hadn't. Until tonight. He hoped to hell Duncan
would be grateful.

"Excuse me," he said, tapping her on the shoulder
to get her attention. "Could I have a light?"

She gazed up at him and a flicker of life twinkled in
her eyes for just an instant and then was gone. "Tony

doesn't have any matches at the bar?'' she inquired coolly.

He smiled at her. "He does, but I'm partial to gold lighters."

"So buy one," Meg suggested, and started to turn away. At the last instant, she changed her mind. There was something about this man's blatant approach that appealed to her. She was used to the slick lines, the groping hands, the lingering gazes from men who wore designer clothes and Rolex watches. She did not know how to react to a man in a rumpled sports jacket whose line had been as polished as tarnished silver. Good breeding told her her remark had been more cutting than the man deserved, even though he hardly seemed devastated. She thought she noticed his lips twitching in amusement. Her common sense told her she ought to leave well enough alone. Even if the man hadn't wanted anything more than a light, she sensed a coiled intensity just below the surface that was bound to prove dangerous. She needed no more danger of any sort in her life right now.

She sighed. She hadn't been listening to her common sense in a very long time. She wasn't even sure she had any. The cigarettes were testimony enough to that. She turned back. "Sorry. Here."

She held out the lighter. The man's gaze met hers squarely and she saw something solid, dependable and caring in his expression. Then he grinned and shook his head ruefully.

"Never mind. I'm trying to quit anyway. I just wanted to get your attention."

He'd already done that. She'd sensed him watching her when she was on the dance floor and had been performing for him in an odd sort of way, seeking some sort of reaffirmation of her attractiveness. Apparently it had worked.

"Any particular reason?" she taunted lightly.

"Does a man need a reason to want to meet a beautiful woman? Couldn't we talk?" he suggested. "Maybe over there." He pointed toward a secluded booth.

Meg hesitated, then shook her head. "I don't think so. I'm with my friends."

"But not *a* friend?"

"No," she admitted, and wondered why, now that she'd proven to herself that she was still attractive, she was bothering to prolong this conversation. Lately she'd been more inclined to reduce persistent strangers to stutters with her sarcasm. It was not a trait she felt particularly proud of, but she wondered again if this was the right time to correct it. Her gaze traveled from this man's thick, shaggy dark brown hair to green eyes that twinkled with tiny flecks of gold and on to his mouth and the tiny scar that teased at the corner, ruining the perfection of those sensual lips and at the same time making them all the more provocative. Her pulse fluttered erratically and another tiny sigh escaped her.

He was not classically good-looking like most of the men here with her tonight. He was intriguingly rugged, a little rough around the edges, and there was a wisdom and weariness in his eyes that made an odd

tenderness well up inside her. It reminded her of
someone she hadn't thought about in a very long time.
The expression in those eyes reminded her of her
grandfather.

As a child she'd loved Duncan Blake to distraction,
waiting for those times when he'd come to visit as any
other child anticipates the arrival of Santa Claus. He'd
always really talked to her, even when she was so little
he had to kneel to look her in the eye. More important, he'd always listened, never once teasing her for
being afraid when things were bad. He always left her
feeling stronger.

Sometimes, especially in the last couple of days, she
had wanted to run to Grandfather, to have him tell her
that everything was going to be all right, but twenty-
seven-year-old women did not seek such reassurances. They stood on their own two feet, especially
when they'd made such a dramatic point of escaping
from overly protective parents and living their own
life.

Meg looked back at the man who was still waiting
so patiently beside her chair and suddenly nodded.
Why not? These other people bored her to tears with
their compulsive need for constant excitement. They
weren't bad people. In fact, she'd known most of them
for years, traveled with them to Palm Beach and
Monte Carlo and London, played tennis with the
women and danced with the men. It was only lately
that she'd grown impatient with them. She sometimes
wondered if any of them had read a book since college. Their self-involvement had been irritating her for

months now, but she couldn't bear to be alone. In their own way they cared about her. Still, she thought as she followed Matt across the bar, it was time she spent an evening with someone who could carry on an intelligent conversation.

Matt had watched the play of expressions on Meg's face and knew that he'd passed some sort of internal test. Now the only question was how much to tell her. Did he dare mention her grandfather, or would that send her fleeing straight back to her companions? As they slid into the booth he decided to opt for caution.

"What are you drinking?" he asked.

"Just tell Tony I'll have my usual," she said.

Matt called the order over to the bartender. While they waited for the drinks, he studied her more closely, noting in dismay the puffy circles under her eyes, the pallor in her cheeks, signs of exhaustion he'd missed when her face was animated, rather than in its present stage of repose. If she was partying every night with this crowd, no wonder she looked like death warmed over and no wonder Duncan was worried about her.

Suddenly he realized she was surveying him as candidly as he was her. "Well, what's the verdict?"

"You could use a haircut," she said bluntly. "And that jacket is a disgrace." She tilted her head thoughtfully to one side. "With a little work, you wouldn't be bad."

"Your comments will be duly noted," he replied dryly.

"And ignored?"

"And ignored," he confirmed. "Unless you want to stay in my life and remind me about the haircuts on a regular basis and start picking out my clothes."

She shook her head. "And have you accuse me of nagging? No, thanks. I've taken my shot. You're on your own now."

"Then I guess you're just going to have to get used to my shaggy hair." His expression brightened. "I do have another jacket, though."

"Is it as bad as this one?"

"Actually, it's probably worse," he admitted cheerfully. "It's been laying in the back of the car for the last six months or so on its way to the cleaners."

A smile broke across Meg's face and she chuckled. "You're outrageous."

"I've always thought of myself as quiet, staid and unassuming," he protested, delighted to see the sparkle that came to life in her eyes when she laughed. It was only a shadow of the brightness he'd seen in the photograph, but it was a start. For reasons he wasn't prepared to explore, he suddenly wanted Meg Blake to laugh all the time. No woman her age should look so incredibly sad.

She leaned toward him then and asked in an exaggeratedly conspiratorial whisper, "Who exactly are you?"

He leaned toward her and matched her tone. "Why are you whispering?"

"Since you hadn't introduced yourself, I thought perhaps it was a secret."

"It's no secret. Ask Tony. He and I go way back."

"Oh, really," she said skeptically. "Then why haven't I ever seen you here?"

"You must not come on the right nights."

"I come here every night."

He met her gaze evenly and asked seriously, "Why?"

She seemed suddenly to withdraw, shrugging her shoulders and refusing to meet his gaze. "Why does anyone go to a bar? To drink. Be with people."

"You didn't look as though you were having all that much fun."

"Is that why you came over? To rescue me?"

"Something like that," he said, hoping she didn't realize how close she'd come to hitting the truth.

"Well, Sir Galahad, it wasn't necessary. I was doing just fine."

"Does that mean you'd rather be back with your friends than here with me?" He made the question sound as plaintive as possible.

A grin tugged at the corners of her mouth. "I don't usually hang out with strangers."

"But I'm not a stranger anymore." He held out his hand, enveloping her slender fingers. He felt as though he were cupping a fragile bird, and that protective feeling he'd felt earlier returned in a rush accompanied by far more potent sensations. "I'm Matt Flanagan."

Meg's eyes narrowed for a minute and she tapped a red-tipped nail thoughtfully against her tooth. "Flanagan?"

Oh, hell, he thought. What if her grandfather had talked about him? He had no idea how long the two had been separated or what they'd discussed when they were together. Maybe the old man had told her war stories and if so, Matt would have figured prominently in some of the more recent ones.

"There're a lot of us around," he said quickly. "It's a common Irish name. Now who are you?"

"Meg Blake."

"That's your name," he corrected. "I asked who you are."

"I'm a will-o'-the-wisp, an elusive lady with no past and no future, only the present," she said lightly, but he noticed a sorrow in her eyes that her carefree tone couldn't counter.

"Then tell me about the present. What's it like for Meg Blake?" he probed, wanting to understand her, needing to get to know her for reasons that went far beyond his commitment to her grandfather, reasons he didn't understand at all. He was tough, disciplined. He'd certainly never been the type to pick up strays.

She grinned at him and there was a hint of the imp that had stared back at him from the picture earlier in the afternoon. "Come dance with me and find out."

He grimaced. "Have mercy on me. Isn't there some other way?"

"Scared?"

"No, but you should be," he warned as he followed her onto the dance floor.

The music was fast and throbbed with a heavy beat. Dancing was not Matt's forte. He had two left feet and, it sometimes seemed, a third one that managed to get in the way of the other two. Still he couldn't have refused the request. The only time all night that Meg had looked happy had been on the dance floor.

He barely moved in time to the music, his eyes drinking in the sight as she writhed her slim body before him, taunting him with her sensuality. Then their eyes met and she suddenly laughed—a light, joyful sound that made the music seem dull and lifeless.

"You're hopeless, Flanagan," she teased as the song ended and a slower one replaced it. She moved into his arms, her fingers resting lightly on his neck, tangling in the hair she thought was too long. "This is probably more your speed."

He promptly stepped on her foot and scowled. "Sorry. Maybe not."

She snuggled even more tightly against him and a beat far wilder than any on the stereo started up in his chest. A light scent of spring flowers surrounded him, arousing images of stolen kisses in a shadowed garden.

"Just sway," she suggested, liking the way she felt in Matt Flanagan's embrace. He held her cautiously, as though she were something precious. His actions reminded her of pictures she'd seen of new fathers with their babies.

She rested her head against his chest and felt the staccato beat of his heart. He caught his breath and she distractedly realized that his response was escalating beyond the casualness she permitted among men she'd known far longer than Matt. She felt his body tense, felt his hard imprint against her and even though she knew she should move away for both their sakes, she couldn't do it. She wanted to stay right where she was—in the strong arms of this stranger.

It might only be a temporary illusion, but it was the first time she'd felt safe in a very long time. She wanted desperately to cling to the sensation for as long as it lasted.

Two

Let's get out of here," Matt said urgently. If he didn't quickly get Meg Blake out of his arms, he was not going to be responsible for his actions. They'd be very predictable, considering how he'd reacted just to an old, childhood snapshot. The complex, very feminine and grown-up reality snuggled provocatively next to him was even more intoxicating.

She grinned up at him. "And go where?" she asked with an impish gleam in her eyes.

"My place," he suggested, then just as quickly scowled and countered, "forget that. Your place."

"Why not your place?" she teased. "Is it as big a disaster as I might expect?"

"No," he retorted. "I have a cleaning lady once a month who ploughs a clear path through the rubble. She was just there yesterday."

"Then what's the problem?"

"If I take you to my place, I won't let you leave," he admitted honestly.

"So? I'll still respect you in the morning."

He sucked in his breath at what she was so clearly and casually offering, but he shook his head sorrowfully and gently touched a finger to her chin. Her skin felt like cool satin and it was all he could do to keep his mind on what he had to say. He wanted to linger with her in his embrace, to warm her until passion exploded into a million white-hot fragments inside them both.

He didn't dare.

"Thanks," he said solemnly, his reluctance evident. He met her questioning gaze directly. "But I wouldn't respect me in the morning. I'm taking you home."

"And leaving me on my doorstep with a chaste peck on the cheek?"

"Something like that," he agreed and wondered if, for all his protestations of chivalry, he'd actually be able to stop at that. He had a feeling if he kissed the mysterious, desirable Meg Blake at all, he would never want to stop. Then he'd want to ravish her body, after which Duncan Blake would come after him with a shotgun. Duncan, as he recalled all too well, had terrific aim.

Thinking of Duncan also reminded him that he'd been given a job to do. He needed to find out if Meg was indeed in some sort of danger. There were times that she'd seemed troubled, but not in trouble. She hadn't been casting surreptitious glances over her shoulder. Nor had there been any sign of fear in her eyes, even when he—an unknown quantity—had approached her. Still, there definitely was something amiss. With his years of experience delving into the darkest corners of people's lives, he could sense it, and he owed it to the old man to check it out more thoroughly. He hoped more than anything that he and Duncan were both wrong.

"Maybe I'll even come in for coffee," he suggested, and was delighted that the idea drew a satisfied grin.

"That's a start. We'll loosen you up yet, Flanagan," she said happily.

She grabbed her jacket off the back of her chair, picked up her purse and waved good-night to her friends. Matt noted that most of them barely acknowledged her departure. Nice group, he thought angrily. She could be leaving with Jack the Ripper, for all the attention they'd paid. Why did a savvy, beautiful woman like Meg hang out with a crowd like this?

"You have a car parked around here?" he asked.

"Nope. I live up the street. I walked."

He scowled at her as they started up the block. He turned the collar of his jacket up against the wind, then grumbled, "Do you always walk around at this hour of the night by yourself?"

She grinned at his protective tone. "No. I walked here at eight o'clock by myself. Now I'm with you."

"And if I weren't here?"

"One of the others would drop me off. I'm not as reckless as you're probably imagining."

"Why would I imagine that?" he retorted dryly.

"I don't even know you and I did invite myself to spend the night at your place."

"So you did." He relaxed finally and grinned. The scar at the corner of his mouth became a wicked dimple. "I just considered that extremely good judgment on your part."

"But you turned me down."

"That's why it was such good judgment."

"Oh, the ego of the man," she groaned as they walked in the door of a faded brick town house with ivy curling up the sides. A sleepy Irish setter with hair only a shade redder than Meg's limped into the hallway to greet her, its tail wagging a slow-motion welcome.

"Did you hear the man, Ginger?" she asked, bending down to scratch the aging dog behind its ear. "He is the epitome of conceit."

Matt's brow arched quizzically and he gazed pointedly at the dog. "Ginger?"

"I name all my pets Ginger," she explained very seriously. "The first one was an orange-and-white cat, who kept dropping by to eat. I finally adopted her. When she died, there was a canary. I'd always wanted a canary to sing me awake in the morning, but I figured it wasn't wise with the first Ginger around. She was a very aggressive cat. Then when the bird died, I got this Ginger. That was two years ago. I rescued her from the pound. I think she's very old, though she's not telling."

"I see. What do you plan on getting next?"

She clamped her hands over the dog's ears and gave him a fierce scowl, though her eyes were filled with laughter. "Hush. You probably talked about the replacement you had in mind, while you were still married, didn't you?"

He laughed. "Sorry. What makes you think I was ever married?"

"You're too appealing not to have been."

"Appealing?"

"You know, rugged masculinity mixed with boyish charm. It's a combination most women can't resist. Even when they know it won't be appreciated, women want to take care of men like you."

"See that they get their hair cut?" he teased.

"Exactly."

"But not you."

"Nope," she said decisively. "I told you I've taken my only crack at it. You can let your hair grow down to your waist for all I care. You're also avoiding the issue."

"What issue?"

"Have you been married?"

"Not recently."

"But you were?"

"A long time ago," he said, trying to bring an image of Paula to mind. It wouldn't come. They'd been so young and it hadn't lasted beyond his first leave from the army, when he'd found her in bed with another man. She'd been too young to tolerate the separations, and he'd been too foolish, too determined to save the world to prevent them. "It seems like another lifetime."

"Out of sight, out of mind, huh?" she said all too accurately. "Remind me not to stay out of your sight too long. Do you want a drink or are you about to make a discreet exit?"

"How about that coffee we talked about?" he suggested, deciding that she drank far more than was good for her. He had no right to challenge her on it, but maybe he could change her by setting a better example than her so-called friends. Better yet he could find out what demons led her to drink in the first place and banish them forever.

"Coffee, it is," she agreed, "But I have to warn you, some very macho men have been known to fall to their knees and weep over my coffee."

"It's that good?"

"No, it's that awful," she confessed with a laugh. "I don't drink the stuff, so I have no idea if what I'm making is any good. It's usually too strong or too weak, depending on which it was the last time I made it. If it was too strong, I leave out a couple of scoops the next time. If it was too weak, I throw in a couple more."

Matt shuddered. He considered coffee brewing to be an art form. "Why don't I make it?"

Meg nodded in satisfaction. "I thought you'd see it that way."

"What about you?"

"Nothing for me. I'm floating now."

Floating in more ways than one, she realized. Being with Matt was just as dangerous as she'd anticipated. She couldn't afford any involvements now. It wouldn't be fair. She could tell that Matt Flanagan was the steady, dependable type who would never take advantage of a woman. Otherwise, he would have taken her up on her offer to go home with him, an offer that had astonished her as much as it had him. But for a fleeting moment she had badly wanted to know the joy of being with a thoughtful, considerate man like Matt. Fortunately, Matt's common sense had prevailed and kept her from making a terrible mistake.

As much as she might wish it were otherwise, this relationship must end before it ever gets started, she reminded herself sternly. They would talk for a while, keeping the loneliness at bay. Matt would kiss her good-night at the door and that would be the end of it. Over the years she'd become very good at quick endings, though she had a feeling tonight's would be one that lingered with her far after the fact.

She liked what she'd seen of Matt Flanagan. He had a mile-wide streak of integrity, a quiet sense of humor and a fierce protectiveness that made her feel very much a woman. It was the latter that reinforced her faltering determination to send him on his way. In trying to protect her, to slay her dragons, in the end he would be the one hurt and she wouldn't allow that to happen.

She sat down at the round, antique oak table in her airy, cheerful kitchen and watched as he puttered about making the coffee. For a man who virtually reeked of the rugged outdoors, he was amazingly at home in the kitchen. He should have been clumsy, but he wasn't. Every movement projected a precise efficiency and deft assurance. He probably fixed terrific breakfasts, she decided wistfully and was sorry once more that he wouldn't be around in the morning to make one for her—sort of a last meal for the condemned woman.

Stop it, Meg, she warned herself. Stop it or you'll have yourself bawling and then he'll never leave. She guessed Matt was the type who'd stay until her tears dried and then remain longer to find out what had caused them. He'd persist until she told him everything and this was something she'd vowed to get through on her own.

"What are you thinking about?" he said softly.

"Oh, dragons and rainbows and butterflies."

He shook his head and scowled at her. "Can't you ever be serious?"

"I try not to be," she said, remembering again how being serious hurt. It hurt like hell, especially these days. She wanted to surround herself with laughter. She gave him a dazzling smile. "Now tell me about yourself, Matt Flanagan, and don't leave anything out."

"What would you like to know?"

"I'd like to know what you were like as a little boy, what kind of toys you had, when you kissed a girl for the first time, where you went to school, what you do with yourself when you're not bumming cigarettes you don't want, your philosophy of life."

"All the easy stuff," he teased, and she felt the dark cloud over her head begin to lift and slowly float away.

He talked to her for hours, far into the night, until she knew that his mother had despaired of ever seeing him without cuts and scrapes, that his father had wanted him to be a lawyer. He took his Aunt Nell peppermint candy at least once a month, and his first girlfriend had been named Marylou and she'd had freckles and pigtails and a right hook that could deck half the boys in school.

Meg was fascinated by the twinkle in his eyes as he recalled Marylou. She was also just the tiniest bit jealous. "She sounds like just your type."

"She was. I was very sorry to lose her. She moved to Omaha and was lost to me forever."

"There are planes to Omaha."

"Not when you're twelve and your allowance is only two dollars a week."

Meg's jealousy fled and she giggled at the image of a twelve-year-old boy chasing across the country after the freckle-faced girl of his dreams. "If you'd really loved her that would not have stood in your way," she proclaimed very seriously.

"Then I guess it must have been infatuation. I'll stop pining away for her now." He gazed into her eyes and she felt her heart skip a beat. "What about you? For instance, how did you chip that tooth? I've been wondering about it ever since..." There was an odd little hesitation in his voice and she studied him curiously.

"...ever since you first smiled at me," he finally concluded.

Meg remembered that accident only too well. "I was trying to escape," she said, not stopping to think how that would sound.

Matt's eyes widened predictably. "Escape?"

"Sounds dramatic, doesn't it? It really wasn't. I'd been sent to my room, but I had other plans. I climbed out my window and tried to crawl down the rose trellis. I accidentally grabbed onto a thorn and the damn thing hurt so bad, I let go of the trellis and fell. My parents were furious. They'd just spent thousands of dollars for orthodontic work and the braces had only been off for a week. For once they were more upset by what I'd done to my tooth than they were by my attempt to sneak out."

"Did you get along with your parents?"

Meg shrugged. It was a question not easily answered. She'd loved her parents and they'd loved her. In fact, they'd loved her so much they'd virtually smothered her. That escape out the window had been only one of many futile attempts to get away. She'd made a far more complete break a few years ago. There were still nights when that awful fight between them haunted her.

"We had our differences," she summed up now, not wanting to get into a more detailed examination of the strained relationship. Even after all this time, it hurt to remember the expression of betrayal in their eyes.

Her father had been furious. Her mother had seemed so very, very sad.

"And now?"

"We still do."

"Any other family?" Matt probed cautiously, knowing he was treading on thin ice. He was listening for the cracks. He heard the first one as shutters slammed closed over her eyes, effectively ending their growing rapport.

"I'd rather not talk about my family, if you don't mind," she said tightly, then deftly changed the subject. "You still haven't told me what you do for a living."

He decided he'd better allow her the evasion. Then, as he thought about an answer to her question, he reminded himself that one should always stick close to the truth. It was a maxim he'd learned long ago. It prevented having to explain the lies later. More important, he wanted as few lies as possible between him and this woman. For reasons he didn't yet totally understand, he wanted very badly for her to trust him.

"I'm a private investigator."

Meg's blue eyes suddenly filled with laughter again and she slapped a hand to her forehead, the gold bracelets on her wrist tinkling merrily. "Of course. That's where I've heard your name before."

Oh, my God, he thought, here it comes. "It is?" he said weakly.

"Bunny Townsend."

Matt felt his head spinning, though he wasn't sure whether the effect was caused by confusion or relief. "Who's Bunny Townsend?"

"You did some investigative work for her when she was getting her divorce."

"And her name's Bunny?" he said incredulously. "No way. I'd remember that name."

"How about Lydia?"

"Ah, of course," he said, an image of a sophisticated bitter woman hell-bent on revenge coming to mind. She would have fit right into that group Meg had been with tonight.

"You helped her nail her husband to the wall. Actually," she confided, "I always felt rather sorry for Carter. Bunny was no prize. If he'd played down and dirty back at her, she wouldn't have walked away from that divorce hearing with a million bucks."

"Maybe he thought it was a small price to pay for his freedom."

"Now that you mention it, he probably did," she agreed. "What are you working on now?"

"A couple of other divorces, a missing husband, that sort of thing," he said, pointedly avoiding the most intriguing case of all—the one involving the lady across from him who made his blood sizzle. He had to gain her confidence before telling her the truth. He also had to get as much information as he could before then because she was very likely to slam a skillet on his head once she found out he'd been sent by her grandfather. He could already tell that there was a definite strain between Meg and her family, and he cursed Duncan Blake for putting him in the middle of the minefield without a map.

"Sounds pretty routine," she said disappointedly.

"It is." He paused, took a deep breath, then asked directly, "Mind if I practice my technique on you?"

"What does that mean?"

"I ask questions. You answer."

"What if I don't like the question?"

He grinned at her. "You seem to be a pretty straightforward lady. I think you'll know what to do, if that happens."

"Okay, ask," she agreed, propping her chin on her hand and gazing into his eyes. Her blue eyes sparkled with interest. Matt's heartbeat picked up and he almost lost his train of thought completely. He wanted to ask her if she believed it was possible to fall in love with a photograph. Instead, he settled for something far less provocative.

"Do you work or is all this—" he gestured at the assortment of modern kitchen accessories and obviously expensive, design-magazine decor "—the spoils of a bad marriage?"

"I work. I do interior design, as a matter of fact. I'm glad you like the kitchen."

"Actually, it intimidates the hell out of me," he confided.

"Oh, dear." Her lips formed a teasing pout. "It's supposed to be homey."

He glanced around skeptically. "Maybe it is, if you're a mechanical genius. Give me an electric cof-

feepot, a cast iron skillet and your basic stove and re-
frigerator."

"No blender? No microwave?"

"Never. In fact, I'd prefer a camp fire."

"I should have guessed. You look like you belong
in the middle of the wilderness."

"I'll take that as a compliment . . . I think."

"It was meant as one. I like men who don't feel the
need to conform."

Matt grinned at her. "Is that another criticism of
my jacket?"

"Certainly not," she denied, but lights were dancing merrily in her eyes.

"See. That wasn't so bad, was it?"

"What wasn't so bad?"

"The first question."

She grinned at him. "No. You're doing okay so far.
Plan to stop while you're ahead?"

"No. I like to live dangerously. For example," he
said, pausing to choose his words carefully, "why
would an attractive, smart lady like you be on the
run?"

Meg's smile faded and was promptly replaced by a
scowl. "On the run? What's that supposed to mean?
It sounds like something you'd ask a criminal, and I
can assure you that other than an occasional traffic
ticket, I'm very law-abiding."

"There are all kinds of reasons to be on the run and
if ever I've met someone who was running from
something or someone, it's you. You get very nervous
when I get too personal. You're wasting your life away

with a bunch of people who aren't worthy of a single minute of your time. By your own admission, you spend every night in one bar or another. And, despite the fact that you very casually agreed to go home with me tonight, I suspect you come home alone most of the time." He regarded her closely. "How am I doing so far?"

"You're pushing, Flanagan," she said tightly. "You have no right to judge my friends. You don't even know them. And how I live my life is none of your business."

Matt sighed and reached for her hand. It was trembling. "I'd like it to be. I like you, Meg. I want to get to know you, but it's a little like trying to get over a wall with barbwire on the top. If you're in some kind of trouble," he said in what he hoped was a casual tone, "I might be able to help."

Meg looked at him peculiarly and began to fit together some of the things she'd learned about Matt Flanagan. The picture she came up with was less reassuring than she would have liked. She frowned at him and hoped like crazy she was wrong.

"Who hired you?" she asked bluntly, removing her hand from the comforting warmth of his grasp. Matt didn't even flinch though she'd expected him to.

"What makes you think anyone hired me?"

"Suddenly it all seems a little too pat. You turn up at the bar tonight, ask me for a light when you don't even smoke, start asking a lot of questions and now you're offering to help me out of some mythical jam

I'm supposed to be in. If I didn't know better, I'd say
my parents put you up to this."

"Up to what?"

"Spying on me."

"I'm not spying. I'm concerned."

"But somebody's paying you to be concerned," she
insisted adamantly.

"No one's paying me," he denied. "Why did you
think your parents might hire someone to check up on
you?"

"What I said was that I knew *better* than to think it
was them. We haven't spoken in several years, not
since I walked out and told them to stay out of my life.
I doubt they'd be resurfacing now." She shook her
head decisively. "No. It has to be someone else."

"Meg, I'm telling you that no one has paid me to be
here. Why are you so paranoid about that anyway? Do
you have something to hide?"

"No, dammit! That's not the point. I trusted you
enough to bring you here, and now I have a feeling
that you're going to betray that trust by running off
and reporting in to someone."

Suddenly it dawned on her. There was only one
other person who might try to pry into her affairs so
blatantly—her grandfather. This was exactly the sort
of outrageous thing Duncan might do. Blast the old
man. Not only was he interfering in something he
didn't understand, but in sending Matt Flanagan he'd
managed to stir up all sorts of feminine reactions in
her, emotions she couldn't afford just now. The only
way to rid herself of those was to toss Matt out on his

ear—quickly, before she could have second thoughts about it.

"Were you in the service, Matt?"

This time he did blink at her unexpected question, but said evenly, "Sure."

"Army?"

He nodded and then she hit him with it.

"You're working for my grandfather, aren't you?"

Matt's face remained impassive. He'd make a helluva poker player. "Your grandfather?" he repeated blankly.

"Duncan Blake. *General* Blake to you, soldier. Does the name mean anything?"

"Every soldier's heard about General Blake."

"Blast it all, Matt, stop avoiding the subject. He hired you, didn't he?"

Matt sighed. "No, he didn't hire me."

Meg felt like crying over his duplicity. She'd expected better of him. But, then, she'd also thought he really liked her. "Please, don't lie to me on top of everything else."

"I'm not lying." She stared at him doubtfully. "Okay. I'm stretching a point. He called in an old debt. He's not paying me. He's worried about you."

"Tell him not to."

"I can't do that."

"Why not?"

"Now that I've met you, seen the way you're living, I'm worried about you, too."

She gestured at the kitchen. "You think there's something wrong with all of this?"

"You know that's not what I mean. Dammit, you *are* in trouble. I can sense it."

"I am not! But if it makes you happy, the two of you can sit on his patio and worry together, as long as you stay away from me," she snapped. "Now, get out."

"Meg, listen to me," Matt implored. "Please let me help. Or go and talk to your grandfather. He wants to help you as much as I do."

Meg heard the tenderness in his voice and wanted to yield, wanted to throw herself into his arms and hold on for dear life, but she wasn't going to. She was going to prove to herself just how strong she could be. It would be the first test of how well she was going to get through the coming months.

"I can handle this by myself."

Matt swooped down on the comment like a bird of prey. "Then there is something to handle?"

"Just get out of here, soldier. The party's over."

She marched to the kitchen door, her back as straight and determined as he'd ever seen Duncan's, her chin set stubbornly. She held the door open and waited.

"Okay," Matt said finally, standing up and going to the door. "I'll leave." He leaned down and brushed a kiss across her forehead before she could protest, then gazed directly into her eyes and saw the mixture of hurt and pride. It wrenched his gut.

"But I'll be back," he promised softly. "Count on it."

He turned back once at the bottom of the steps and caught a glimpse of her face as she shut the door. It might have been a trick of the light, but he could have sworn there were tears glistening on her cheeks. It was all he could do to restrain himself from rushing back and demanding that she start at the beginning and tell him what was going on to make her so miserable. But he knew there was no point in returning tonight. As proud and stubborn as Meg Blake clearly was, she'd only slam the door in his face. He felt like pounding on something himself—maybe Duncan's nose for starters.

Three

___

You blew it!" Duncan exploded, his crystal-clear blue eyes as icy with condemnation as Matt had ever seen them. His voice shook with fury. Matt was unimpressed. "Is that what you're telling me, son? You blew it?" Duncan repeated.

"I'd say that's an understatement," Matt replied, recalling Meg's righteous indignation. "Your granddaughter's temper is everything you said it was."

Duncan sighed and sank down into an overstuffed chair.

"Dammit," he said wearily, all of his bluster now gone. "I told you to go slow. Didn't you learn anything from me? I thought I'd taught you to watch and wait until you had all the facts."

"You also said time was of the essence. I thought I'd get the facts quicker by being direct. I did what I thought was best, sir. I'm sorry."

Duncan waved off the apology. "Regrets are useless, Matt. Now what? We can't drop this, just because you've made a royal mess of things so far. What's your next step?"

A slamming door prevented Matt from responding, which was just as well since his plan wasn't something he especially wanted to discuss with Duncan. He was simply going to plant himself squarely in the middle of Meg's life so that no harm could come to her. His decision was strictly personal and the less said to Duncan about *that* the better. Meg would hardly believe his interest in her was genuine, if her grandfather was consulting on every move he made.

Both men turned just in time to see Meg poised on the threshold, her hair crackling with electricity as it fell down her back in a glorious tangle of curls. Her eyes glittered with angry sparks. She looked, Matt thought as he drew in an unsteady breath, spectacularly beautiful.

"His next step is going to be to stand here and listen while you apologize to him and me for sending him rushing to the rescue," she said to her grandfather. She regarded him accusingly, and Matt noted that pain was still shadowed her eyes. "You had no right."

"I had every right," Duncan corrected softly. "I love you."

"Then you're a coward," she stormed. "If you loved me so much and were so damned concerned, why didn't you come after me yourself? I'll tell you why. You knew exactly how I'd feel about your meddling, so you wanted Mike Hammer here to do your dirty work, didn't you, you son of—''

"Watch you tongue, young lady."

"I learned my bad language from you, you old buzzard."

"That doesn't mean you should use it."

"I only use it when the situation calls for it and this one does. You're a low-down, conniving skunk, Grandfather."

Matt watched as Duncan drew himself up into military bearing. He caught the quick glimmer of amusement in the old man's eyes and wondered if Meg had seen it, as well. He'd suddenly realized that, despite the fireworks last night and just now, there was an extraordinary bond of affection between these two. He wondered more than ever why Meg seemed so determined to stand alone against whatever was happening in her life when she had an ally as formidable as Duncan.

"Matt," Duncan asked formally, "would you leave me alone with my granddaughter now? I gather there are a few things she'd like to say."

"Certainly, sir." He captured Meg's gaze and held it, throwing down a gauntlet of his own to her. "You and I have some business to settle later."

She looked away. "We do not."

"I'll pick you up at seven."

Her lips set stubbornly. "I won't be there."

"Then I'll wait," he promised. He heard her muttered oath and Duncan's quickly suppressed chuckle as he closed the front door behind him.

When Matt had gone, Meg sighed, then faced her grandfather. All of the anger seemed to have drained right out of her. In a way she was filled with relief that her grandfather had taken the first step. She needed him so, but she wasn't sure she'd have been able to admit that.

"Why now? Why after all this time?" she asked softly, not really certain it even mattered. She'd felt stronger just by walking into this familiar room again and seeing Duncan sitting in his favorite armchair, his eyes lighting at the sight of her just as they always had. And Matt. Dammit, she'd been glad to see him, too. As furious as she'd been at the pair of them, her heart had skipped joyfully, obviously not concerned that Matt was a traitor. She tried once more to put the infuriating man out of her mind and waited for Duncan to speak.

"I've always loved you, Granddaughter. You were the one who chose to leave me behind at the same time you walked away from the rest of your family."

"You'd already gone."

He sighed wearily. "It's no wonder you thought that. It was wrong but after your father and I fought, I had to stay away. But I would have come if you'd needed me. You had only to ask."

"I couldn't. I was so sure you'd abandoned me, that you were tired of listening to all my problems. Be-

sides, I had to grow up. To do that, I had to cut all my
ties to the past.''

He nodded. ''I know you did. It was time.''

Meg was surprised. ''You understood that?''

''Of course I did, girl. Do you think I'm blind? I
saw what they were doing to you. That's why your father and I argued. I knew it was only a matter of time
until you'd want to get out and live your own life.
Used to tear me apart watching how they tried to keep
you chained to that house. A bright, pretty girl like
you had a right to some fun, to go out and make
friends, make your own mistakes.'' He watched her
carefully and Meg felt herself shivering under the
knowing scrutiny. ''Made a bundle of them, too,
didn't you?''

She allowed herself a tiny smile. ''A bundle,'' she
agreed.

''Too many, Margaret?'' he asked, and there was a
hint of desperation in his voice.

Her eyes filled with tears. ''I don't know, Grandfather. Maybe so.''

He held out his arms then and she ran into them.
''I'm so scared,'' she said as he patted her on the back,
soothing her just as he had when she was a little girl.
Now, though, the fear didn't vanish quite so easily.
She'd been living with this unbearable knot inside her
for days now, and even her grandfather's comfort
couldn't make it go away.

''I know, child. So am I.'' When her tears had
stopped at last, he said gently, ''Tell me exactly what's
happened. Don't shut me out again, Margaret.''

It was the first time Meg could ever remember her grandfather pleading for anything. She shook her head ruefully. "It's too late for that now."

"What can I do, child? Do you need money? Anything?"

"No. I'm faced with a problem money can't solve. Just tell Matt Flanagan to stay away from me. I don't need him hovering. I've had enough of that in my life."

His eyes twinkled then. "So, that's the way it is," he said, his expression all too knowing.

"Why you cagey old man," she exclaimed, wagging a finger in his face. "You knew exactly what you were doing. Otherwise, you would have come yourself. You want that man around pestering me, don't you?"

Duncan didn't look the least bit guilty. "Let's just say I have my hopes. You wouldn't deny an old man his dreams would you?"

Meg sighed. "I don't want to, grandfather, but I have to this time. Please, if you care about me—for that matter, if you care about him—tell him to forget whatever order you've given."

"If that's what you really want, I'll try, but I doubt I'll have much luck. I saw the way he looked at you. He seems to have grown mighty fond of you already. And, as you've already noticed, Matt Flanagan's tenacious . . . just like you and me."

He certainly was. It was after nine o'clock that night when Meg finally returned home and Matt was waiting on the front steps of the town house. He was hud-

dled on the top step, the collar of that horrible
rumpled jacket turned up against the cold. Meg felt
the tiniest glimmer of guilt, then reminded herself she
was not responsible for the man's stubborn persis-
tence. If he wanted to freeze his buns off, it was not
her doing.

"You're still here," she said flatly, not even bothering to pretend surprise.

"I told you I would be."

She stepped around him and inserted her key in the
lock. "Have you been here since seven?"

"Yes."

"Then I suppose you might as well come on in," she
said ungraciously.

"I can't."

"You can't?" she said, returning to peer down at
him. Green eyes glinted back at her. "Why not, if
you've been waiting all this time?"

"I can't move. Do you have any idea how cold it is
out here? My old bones can't take it."

"Don't give me that act, Matt Flanagan. Your
bones are not that old."

"I'm telling you I must have premature arthritis or
something. Just bring me coffee..." He winced. "No,
forget that, make it tea. You can make tea, can't
you?"

She nodded, repressing a chuckle.

"Then bring me tea every so often. Maybe a sand-
wich now and then. I'll move again in July, when I
thaw out."

She bent over and gazed into his eyes. They stared back at her guilelessly. She didn't trust those eyes of his one bit. She scowled at him fiercely. "Are you lying to me again?"

Matt's heart flipped over as the light, flowery scent of her perfume taunted him. "I've never lied to you," he replied indignantly.

"Last night was one big lie."

"No," he said evenly. "It wasn't. I am worried about you."

Meg sighed. She now knew exactly why her grandfather had picked this particular Sir Galahad to come to her rescue, but understanding only made it worse. Matt was clearly going to be a nuisance. He was really going to care, and that was going to make everything so blasted difficult. Especially since she could feel herself responding to the warmth in his eyes and the compassion in his voice. She was opening up to him, just like a flower to sunlight.

That was why she'd stayed away so long tonight, hoping that her grandfather had been wrong about Matt's tenacity and that she'd misjudged his interest. She'd even convinced herself that if he showed up and she didn't, he'd leave. She should have known better. Any friend of her grandfather's was not likely to be a quitter. In fact, he was likely to relish a good challenge.

She sat down on the step next to Matt and tried appealing to his sense of integrity. Surely he wouldn't persist in this, if he realized he was hurting her.

"Matt, please, give up this crazy idea you have of protecting me from harm. I'm not in any danger and you're just making things more difficult. I have a perfectly fine life at the moment, and there's no room in it for men who get their kicks from rescuing damsels in distress."

"Is that what is happening here?"

"Isn't it? My grandfather taunted you with the notion that his darling Margaret was in trouble and you probably jumped at the chance to rush to the rescue. You get an opportunity to pay him back for whatever he did for you and earn your Boy Scout badge at the same time."

"Actually, I tried to tell him to go to hell."

Her eyes widened. She'd have given anything to witness that. "You did?"

"I said I tried. You know your grandfather. He ignored me. Next thing I knew I was sitting on a bar stool in Georgetown."

"Then get out of this now. It's not too late."

"Oh, but it is."

"Why? I told Grandfather this morning to rescind his stupid order."

"I know. He mentioned it when I talked to him this afternoon."

"And you said?"

"This time I did tell him to go to hell. I'm in this for the duration. Whatever's wrong, I intend to help."

"Oh, damn," Meg moaned.

"Meg?"

"Yes."

"I'm starving. Do you know how to use any of those gadgets in your kitchen?"

"Most of them."

He gazed at her appealingly and she felt something melt inside. Why did the man have to be so irresistible? Why did her heart pound like a jackhammer at the mere sight of him? Why couldn't he have been one of those irresponsible men who scampered like rats from a sinking ship when they sensed a problem? Problems obviously turned Matt Flanagan on. Well, with her he was getting far more than he bargained for.

"You're going to make me beg, aren't you?" he said so pathetically that she finally laughed and shook her head.

"No," she said, standing up and holding out a hand to help him up. She might as well relent now and get it over with. "Come on. I'll fix you dinner, if you'll promise me one thing."

He eyed her warily. "What's that?"

"That you will leave quietly the minute you've been fed."

He shook his head as he darted past her and stepped inside the house. "Sorry, babe. I can't do that."

She glowered at him, her hands on her hips. "For a man whose bones were supposed to be all frozen up, you just moved with amazing agility."

"Army survival training," he retorted with a grin. "Your grandfather taught me."

"What a guy," she said dryly. "Now about the terms of our settlement."

"You fix dinner. I do the dishes."

"And then you leave," she repeated stubbornly.

"And then we talk," he said just as stubbornly.

"Matt, there's nothing to talk about."

"Could we debate that while you fix a nice juicy steak?"

"I don't eat meat."

"I should have known," he said with a groan, trailing behind her into the kitchen.

"I do make a terrific herb-and-cheese omelet with home fried potatoes, though."

"It'll do," he grumbled ungraciously. "Next time we're going out."

"There will be no next time."

"You sound like a broken record."

"So do you," she said as she cracked the eggs into a bowl and added several herbs, then whipped the concoction to a pale yellow frothiness. "Why are you so determined to pursue this? You're off the hook. My grandfather has forgotten whatever debt you owe him."

"That debt will never be fully repaid. He saved my life."

Her head snapped around. "He did? Tell me about it." She looked at him hesitantly. "Or is it something you'd rather not talk about?"

"I'd rather not talk about it."

"I'm sorry. It's still too painful, isn't it?"

"No. It makes me look like a jerk."

She giggled at the absolutely chagrined expression on his face. "Now I have to hear it. Talk, Flanagan."

"And you think I've got a twisted mind," he muttered in disgust. "You get off on war stories."

"With Duncan Blake for a grandfather, did you think I grew up on fairy tales? Now, talk."

"Okay. We were in the jungle in Central America on an unofficial training mission with the Contras. One of the first things you need to learn is that in a situation like that you should always be aware of what's around you. You listen, observe, wait."

"I think I see the trouble spot already."

"Don't be a wise guy. Do you want to hear this story or not?"

"Oh, I want to hear it. I can hardly wait."

He glowered at her. "We were scattered through the hills, when I suddenly heard a noise, the snapping of a twig, something. Instead of protecting myself until I knew for sure what was happening, I stalked in the direction of the noise to blast the Contra for being too careless."

"Only it wasn't a Contra," Meg guessed.

"Bingo. I found myself staring down the barrel of a very nasty gun. The kid holding it did not appear friendly or overly confident. They're the most dangerous kind. Fortunately, your grandfather had heard the same noise that I had, only he'd followed procedure and approached cautiously. He blew the gun out of the kid's hand just as he pulled the trigger. The shot missed me by inches."

"So now you figure it's up to you to save me, just the way my grandfather rescued you?"

His eyes burned with an intensity that stunned her. "This has nothing to do with your grandfather. Now this is between you and me. It has been since the first minute I saw you," he said with a solemnity that took her breath away.

"But why, Matt? I don't understand. You don't even know me."

He shook his head and before she realized what was happening, he'd wrapped his arm around her waist and pulled her into his lap. White hot tendrils of heat curled along her spine. "For a smart lady, you certainly are slow about some things."

"For a man who professed to be old and creaky, you have mighty quick reflexes."

There was a triumphant spark of satisfaction in his eyes as he muttered, "Don't I, though? Better late than never."

Then he was urging her head down until their lips met, barely touching at first, his warm and soft and gentle and, therefore, all the more tempting. It was Meg who was unable to bear the tenderness, Meg who sent the kiss spiraling into a whirlwind of passion by opening her mouth and letting the tip of her tongue brush across his lips until he moaned and kissed her thoroughly. The caress was like silk sliding slowly across velvet, tenderly snagged again and again. She was breathless when he pulled away at last, breathless and scared.

This wasn't what she wanted, she kept telling herself, but she knew it wasn't true. She wanted this man's passion and potency as she'd wanted no other's. She could feel his strength seeping into her, making her strong again.

Not now, her head screamed.

Especially now, her heart shouted right back.

It was a battle she'd fought often, but never with the stakes so high. Still, her head won and with a deep, shuddering sigh she stood up and turned her back, literally and figuratively, on Matt. With trembling hands, she poured the eggs into a skillet and concentrated on making the omelet. The silence in the room crackled with tension so thick she thought she might scream—or throw herself straight back into Matt's arms—if it didn't end.

"I'll never leave now," he said so quietly that at first she wasn't even sure she'd heard him speak.

Her hands gripped the spatula so tightly her knuckles turned white. "You have to," she protested, but her will to fight the inevitable was growing progressively weaker. "I don't want a man in my life who only feels sorry for me."

Matt's answering laugh was harsh. "Is that what you think I feel?"

"Isn't it?"

"What I feel for you goes deeper than anything I've ever felt for a woman before and it has nothing to do with pity, believe me. I don't know what's going on between us and, to tell you the truth, it scares the hell out of me, but I'm not going to run from it."

He waited until she'd put their plates on the table and had seated herself across from him before he asked gently, "Are you?"

She closed her eyes for a moment as though she could only find composure by avoiding his gaze. When she opened them, she said firmly, "Yes, Matt, I am."

He regarded her in astonishment. He had expected her to admit finally that she was feeling exactly the same way he was. Her body certainly bore testament to this. She had responded to his kiss more passionately then he'd dared hope. How could she deny that?

"It's not what I want," she insisted.

"For someone so hung up on honesty, I'm surprised at you," he taunted. "You're either lying to me or to yourself. You don't want to end this any more than I do. We owe it to ourselves to explore these feelings."

As the futile argument raged on and the hour grew later, Meg could feel herself getting shakier, her skin growing cold and clammy. He had to go now or he would find out the truth.

"Dammit," she finally exploded in desperation. "Why the hell don't you just leave? Can't you get it through that egotistical skull of yours that I don't want you here?"

"I don't believe that."

"Believe it," she retorted, jumping up and racing upstairs to the bathroom. She slammed the door behind her and locked it. Her hand trembling, she reached into the medicine cabinet just as Matt started pounding on the door.

"Meg, please, come out of there and talk to me. Hiding is not going to solve this."

"I am not hiding." She said each word emphatically.

"If you don't open this door, I'll break it down," he threatened and she could tell from the strain in his voice that he meant it.

"Matt, please," she pleaded, "Leave well enough alone. Go away."

Suddenly the door burst open and Meg whirled around, her hands dropping to her side.

"How dare you? Get out," she said, her eyes filled with fury at his invasion of her privacy. But Matt was looking beyond her, his own eyes widening with shock.

"My God," he said softly, dismayed green eyes shifting from the needles on the shelf in the medicine cabinet to meet her gaze. "Drugs? I never even thought... That's what your grandfather was worried about, wasn't it? He knew."

Every stupid, unthinking incident from the past came flooding back, making her shake so badly she had to sit down. She balled her hands into fists to still the trembling. Damn him! And damn this disease!

"He knew, but it's not what you think, you Neanderthal!" she shouted furiously, stunned that he could think such a thing about her. "I'm a diabetic and if you'll read the label on the bottles next to those needles..." She paused and regarded him scathingly. "You can read, can't you?"

Matt paled as she lashed out at him and the scar at the corner of his mouth turned white. His mounting anger made her shudder, but she was beyond caring, beyond hurt. She'd wanted so badly to believe in him, but, just as she had feared, he was like all the others. None of them could cope with her diabetes. It would always be there, robbing her of a normal life, robbing her of love.

When she spoke again, her voice was quiet and calm and icy cold. "The only *drug* I use is my insulin."

Relief was evident in the change of expression on his troubled features. Relief and something else, something she interpreted as pity.

"Oh, babe, I'm sorry. I had no idea. I'm sorry."

"Sorry won't do it," she said wearily. "Not now. Just get the hell out of my house! I need to take my shot and I'd like very much to do it in private."

"Meg..."

"Please, Matt. Just go."

He turned at last and walked slowly down the stairs. When he was gone, she picked up the needle, filled it and gave herself the injection. Then she flung the needle across the room, tears streaming down her face.

Four

———

Matt retreated to the living room, still shaken by the panic that had flashed through him when he'd burst into the bathroom. As much as he hadn't wanted to believe what he was seeing, for a horrible moment he'd felt that it made an awful kind of sense. Drug addiction would have explained the hopelessness he'd noticed in Meg's eyes the seemingly wild, irresponsible friends she'd chosen.

But the fact that she had diabetes didn't explain anything. Millions of people had the disease, from what little he knew. It wasn't a killer, like cancer or heart disease. It didn't carry any sort of social stigma. Meg was lucky.

Or was she? There was probably a lot more about diabetes that he didn't know, maybe even enough to create this aura of fear that surrounded her. If her illness was serious after all, it would certainly explain her grandfather's concern. Yet something didn't make sense. Perhaps the discovery of her condition had simply thrown him off-track.

He sighed and tried to relax, unconsciously pulling the unopened pack of cigarettes from his pocket. He'd torn off the cellophane wrapper before he realized what he was doing and determinedly put the pack back in his pocket.

He stood up and began pacing, twisting the information he had around in his head, hoping to discover some answers. But only Meg had the answers and he had no idea if she would be willing to share them. All he could do now was wait, and Matt had never been very good at that.

When Meg finally returned downstairs, she stood in the doorway of the living room, her back straight and proud and a defiant expression on her face. Though her eyes were puffy and red from crying, he was impressed by her strength. She was Duncan's granddaughter all right. Despite her tough demeanor, he had never wanted more to take a woman in his arms and simply hold her. He knew, though, she'd never allow it.

"I thought I'd asked you to leave," she said stiffly.

"Sorry. I couldn't do that," he said, idly turning a small, rounded, abstract sculpture over and over in his massive hands. The smooth granite felt cool. The action had the same soothing effect he'd heard the Greeks found in their worry beads. It didn't work as well as smoking, but at least it wouldn't kill him. If the flare of fury in Meg's eyes was anything to go by, however, she still might.

"Exactly why couldn't you go? Is your arthritis acting up again?" she asked, her voice dripping sarcasm.

"Actually, I seem to have my foot stuck in my mouth." He looked up at her winningly. Her harsh expression didn't waver. Her lips were compressed into an unforgiving frown. "Meg, I am sorry. I didn't understand."

"No, you just blindly jumped to the conclusion that I was a hardened drug user. That says a lot about your respect for me, doesn't it?"

He sighed. "Look, I know I've botched this up. I reacted instinctively. In my business, more often than not needles equate with drugs. And although my feelings for you are very strong, we really don't know each other all that well. I knew that your grandfather was worried about something that was happening to you. He refused to explain what. When I saw those syringes, I jumped to all the wrong conclusions. Diabetes never even occurred to me. I've never known anyone who had it."

He gazed at her pleadingly. "Trust me, Meg. I am sorry. Please, won't you talk to me?"

Meg closed her eyes, then sighed and opened them slowly. He couldn't stand the pain he saw shadowing that brilliant blue. It was as though a cloud had drifted across a sunlit sky.

"How do you expect me to trust you, when you obviously don't trust me?" she said softly.

"I'm still here, aren't I? Doesn't that tell you anything?"

"It says that you're very loyal to my grandfather. Or perhaps you're just curious."

"Curious?" he repeated incredulously.

"Why not? That is your business, isn't it? Snooping around in other people's lives—including mine."

"Dammit, Meg," Matt snapped, then struggled for control. Yelling at her wasn't the answer. She'd only withdraw even further. He deliberately softened his voice. "How many times do you want me to say I'm sorry? I didn't want to believe it. Everything inside me shouted that I was crazy, but I couldn't ignore what I was seeing. You'll never know how relieved I am that I was wrong. The thought of you destroying yourself that way terrified me. Despite what you think, I care about you."

He patted the sofa next to him. "Please. Sit here and tell me about it. Help me to understand."

When she didn't move, he put the sculpture aside, stood up and went to her, taking her hand in his. It was cold as ice, but she didn't pull away. "Please."

Something tore loose inside Meg at the simplicity of Matt's request. He sounded so damn sincere, and at last, unable to ignore that sincerity, she nodded and went with him to the sofa. But she sat down at the far end, not wanting to be close to him, afraid of where closeness might lead. Her anger over his misunderstanding had begun to fade and she was filled with

conflicting emotions. One part of her felt that it would
be better to tell him everything and have him leave her
because of it. No matter how badly she wanted him to
stay, nothing had really changed. This was still no time
for her to be drawing a man into the tangled web of
her life. But, oh, how she wanted to.

She regarded Matt through lowered lashes, noted
the warmth and concern in his expression. Although
he was slouched into a relaxed position, his body
exuded energy and attentiveness. A soft, wistful sigh
escaped. God, how she wished things could be different. He was someone she could count on. Even during that brief instant when he'd labelled her as a drug
addict she'd seen compassion and fear, not horror in
his eyes. He would have stayed with her, helped her,
even if the worst had been true.

"Are you okay?" he asked gently now.

"Yes."

"Then tell me why your diabetes is something you
try to hide. Why didn't you just tell me about it before you went upstairs?"

Meg wasn't sure how to begin. Even now, after all
these of living with the disease, she still found it painful to talk about it.

"I couldn't. I didn't know how you'd react."

"For heaven's sakes, it isn't some awful social disease."

"Sometimes I wonder if it isn't worse."

"Why?"

"From the time I found out I had diabetes, when I
was barely a teenager, I've never felt as though I were

the one in control of my life," she told him at last. "It was always the diabetes running things. I had to eat at a certain time, take my shots, plan ahead if I wanted to do something strenuous. It was something that never went away."

Her eyes met his. "Do you have any idea what it's like for a kid to have to calculate the impact of every last thing on her body? I couldn't even have a milk shake after school without scheduling it. Sometimes I feel as though I've never done a spontaneous thing in my life."

Matt's expression grew puzzled. "What's wrong?" she asked.

"If you have to be so careful, what about the smoking and drinking?"

She winced and gave him a rueful little half smile. "You would pick up on that. I shouldn't be smoking. I need to stop. As for drinking, I don't."

"But I saw you."

"You saw me drinking ginger ale . . . my usual."

"Thank God," he muttered and Meg grinned.

"You were worried I was an alcoholic on top of everything?"

"Well, it did seem to me that you were drinking far too much and those friends of yours . . ." He shuddered.

"But you stuck around anyway," she said in amazement. "You really do feel indebted to my grandfather."

"No, angel. Despite the error of your ways, I liked what I saw, as you perfectly well know. I'll repeat it one last time: this has stopped having anything to do with Duncan. Now tell me more about the diabetes.''

"I suppose the worst thing was the impact it had on my friends. When I first found out, I told a few of them, but I realized fairly quickly that it seemed to scare them. I even passed out a few times and that certainly didn't help. Once they knew, once they'd seen that happen, they didn't come around quite so often. By the time I went on to high school and met new people, I had learned not to mention it.''

"It must have been awful for you.''

"Not awful. I just grew up very quickly. I had to learn to be responsible at a time when other kids were just having fun. I wanted so badly to be like other kids. Adolescence is bad enough without feeling that you're so very, very different.''

"Were your parents supportive?''

She grimaced. "In their own way, I suppose they meant to be, but it was as if they thought I had a terminal illness. I always felt they were ashamed somehow that they'd created this imperfect child. Now that I'm older and have been away for awhile I think maybe they were just worried about me and wanted to protect me from being hurt.''

"What did they do?''

"They smothered me. One or the other of them seemed to be with me every minute, watching over me, making sure I took my medicine on schedule, seeing that I got my rest.''

He grinned in sudden understanding. "Ah, so that's what brought on the great escape!''

"Exactly."

"I'm glad you fell off that trellis," he said, smiling at her so tenderly that Meg felt wrapped in sunshine. It was almost unbearable to think about giving that feeling up.

"Do you have some slightly sadistic tendencies?" she retorted lightly.

"No. I love that chipped tooth. No one should have an absolutely perfect face. It's intimidating."

"Then I suppose I should thank my parents for forcing me to find an escape route after all."

"I'll thank them, when I meet them."

Her smile froze. "You won't be meeting them."

"Why not?"

"We don't communicate. The minute I graduated from college and got a job, I packed my bags and moved out. I desperately needed to prove that I could manage my own life."

"Surely you've more than proved that now. You have a successful career, friends."

"I suppose. But it's hard to go back again. My father especially is very bitter. I did try to call once a couple of years ago. He hung up on me." She said it matter-of-factly, but Matt saw the anguish in her eyes.

"Does this have anything to do with the rift between him and your grandfather?"

"Everything, though I never knew it until this morning. Apparently several years before I left, Grandfather tried to get them to ease up, but they wouldn't hear of it. They finally told him their house was one place where he couldn't play general and to stay the hell away. He did. Until today, I thought he'd abandoned me.''

"How could you ever think that? It's so obvious that your grandfather loves you very much."

"I realize that now. He always understood how I felt, how important it was for me to feel normal. He was always so strong and I wanted to be just like him. I didn't think I'd ever be that brave, though, because I was so terribly afraid."

"Fear makes you strong," Matt said. "As long as you don't run from it."

Meg grinned at him. "You sound exactly like Grandfather."

"There are worse things you could say about me." He inched toward her and held out his hand. She shook her head.

"Matt, don't get the wrong idea. This disease isn't easy. There's still time for you to run from it, from me. I wouldn't blame you. In fact, I think you should. If I were you, I'd run like hell."

"Then I guess it's a good thing you're not me, isn't it?" he said, moving closer still. He reached up and caressed her cheek, the light touch warm and reassuring. It also sent wonderful little tingles scampering over her body. "I'm not afraid, Meg. Together, I think we could face just about anything."

Meg let out the breath she'd been holding with a soft whoosh of relief. Tonight, she thought. Just let me have tonight with this wonderful, gentle man and I'll never ask for another thing.

Her eyes met his hesitantly at first, then more boldly. "I'm glad. Does that mean that this time you're staying?"

"If you'll have me."

"I'll have you."

"Then come over here."

She shook her head. "Not here," she said, standing and holding out her hand. He took it, his strong fingers enveloping her still-shaking ones. She held on tightly and led him up the stairs to her room, which was dominated by a king-size bed that normally made her feel just a little lost and lonely. Tonight she knew it wouldn't feel that way at all. Already Matt's presence was bringing warmth and excitement to a room that she usually thought of as nothing more than a place to sleep.

When he reached for the light switch, she stopped him. "Don't," she whispered. "I want to make love to you in the moonlight. I want it to be just like a wonderful romantic fantasy."

"But this is real," he argued. "We're two flesh and blood people who need each other very much. Don't try to pretend it's just a dream."

"If it's a dream, I won't feel quite so bad when it's over," she said wistfully.

"Oh, babe," Matt moaned softly, gathering her into his arms. "It's not ever going to be over."

"Ssh. Don't make promises you can't keep. Just give me tonight."

Matt's fingers brushed gently across her lips, as his eyes held hers. He could feel an intense shudder sweep through her and a white-hot flare of desire ripped through him and settled in his loins. When she drew his exploring finger into her mouth, sucking gently, an answering shudder rocked through him.

He trailed the moistened finger along her neck, finding the racing pulse, hesitating as if he could learn the frantic rhythm of her heartbeat and match it. He wanted so badly to give her pleasure, to share with her sensation after sensation until the intensity was too much for either of them to bear. He wanted to help her put all of the bad memories behind, to taste the sweetness of her skin and feel her tongue running over the roughness of his flesh. He wanted to bury himself in her velvet softness and feel the flames of passion roaring through his veins. He wanted all of that and he began it with just a touch, then followed it with a kiss.

Their lips played a tender, teasing game of cat and mouse until neither of them could stand it another instant. Matt's body was on fire and only Meg could put out the flames. He dipped his tongue inside her mouth, heard the low moan in her throat as she tilted her hips reflexively into the cradle of his. Blood surged to his abdomen and he knew Meg realized exactly what she was doing to him. She rubbed against him, increasing the torment. He pulled away, drawing a ragged breath.

"Slow down, babe, or I won't be able to control myself."

"I don't want you to control yourself. I want you to love me until I can't bear it for another second. I want to feel alive,'' she said, running her fingernails provocatively along his neck, then tangling her fingers in the curls of hair on his chest. She opened the remaining buttons and pulled his shirt free of his pants. Her eyes explored as boldly as her hands.

''Well?'' she demanded impishly. ''Do I have to do this all by myself?''

''Actually, you're doing just fine,'' he said. ''I thought maybe we could take turns. You finish, then I'll start.''

''I think it works better if we're in this together.''

''Oh, we will be,'' he promised, a burning light sparkling in his green eyes. ''Eventually.''

''If you say so,'' she said. She dipped her head and ran her tongue around his hard masculine nipple, relishing the sharp gasp of breath that confirmed her effect on him. She urged him backward until his knees caught the edge of the bed and he fell down. Laughing, she tumbled on top of him, holding his arms above his head and raining kisses along his throat and chest.

Meg loved the feel of his hard body beneath hers. The textures, so different from her own, excited her, reminded her of the essence of the differences between the sexes. They were differences to be treasured, explored. She ran her hands over Matt's exquisite body, dipping her fingers daringly below the waistband of his pants, then rubbing her hand along the fabric stretched taut between his thighs. He groaned and slid his hands inside her sweater, skimming along her already heated flesh to find the hardened tips of her breasts. He flicked the sensitive buds with his nails, sending spasms of pleasure ricocheting through her.

"Oh, Matt, that feels so good," she said wriggling against him. "I want to feel your touch everywhere."

"Soon, Meg." He slipped his hands to her bottom, holding her still against him. "I have to ask you something first."

Puzzled, she waited, almost terrified that for some reason he would decide to stop.

"Is this okay? Are you protected?"

She breathed a sigh of relief and felt new waves of delight that he would be so cautious with her. "It's okay," she murmured, her fingers tracing an outline of his mouth, coming to rest on the scar that was like an exclamation point on his emotions. When he smiled, it gave him a devilish, rakish air. When he was angry, it made him appear fierce. Now it somehow seemed to emphasize his solemn gentleness.

He nodded and his lips curved into a grin. "That's good, because I'm not sure I could have stopped."

"You could have," she said with certainty. "That's the kind of man you are, Matt Flanagan. And that's the reason I want you to make love with me."

She shifted against him. "Now, please," she added with urgency.

"Now," he agreed and began slowly stripping away her clothes, pausing only to caress each new expanse of bare flesh, to stroke until fire roared in her veins and her body was arching and twisting, first into and then away from his unbearably exquisite touch. She ached to feel him inside her, to know the feeling of completion that only a joining with someone like Matt could bring.

She pushed his shirt off his shoulders, then reached for the buckle of his pants. Her movements were frenzied, her body desperate for release, but she didn't want to let go until she could share it with him. First times were rarely this special. True pleasure usually required an intimate knowledge of the other person, but somehow she and Matt had that knowledge instinctively.

When at last he was free of his clothes and braced over her, she knew a feeling of incredible anticipation. His eyes locked with hers, stared into the depths of her soul and read her hidden desires. Then, with a slow, deliberately taunting thrust, he fulfilled them, completing her as no other man ever had, possibly because he alone knew at least some of her secrets.

As their bodies danced in the slow tempo of an ancient rite, arching together, then pulling away, then coming together again, the wisps of fire inside Meg were fanned into an all-consuming blaze. She was burning up from the inside out, her body covered with a sheen of perspiration that sensitized her skin all the more to Matt's relentless touch.

Their rhythm picked up, forcing them into the inferno of sensations that promised them a spectacular release. The feelings were so intense, Meg thought she would die if it didn't end soon and yet she moved into Matt's urgent strokes, her body demanding that she take everything he had to offer. Her mind no longer had any control over what was happening. It was just Matt, urging her on with a husky crooning and demanding kisses that drove her to a wild thrashing beneath him.

His fingers were on her breasts, his tongue deep in her mouth, when she felt him explode inside her, the wicked rocking of his body sending her over the edge into a fantasy more passionate than anything she could ever have dreamed.

It was magic.

It was joy.

In fact, for a shattering moment Meg felt she was on the brink of capturing the essence of life.

Five

Meg's feelings of sheer exhilaration vanished with the dawn. Once more she was struck by uncertainty. As incredible as the night had been, it was wrong of her to encourage a relationship with someone as gentle and sensitive as Matt. She had taken last night selfishly and it was a memory she would hold on to forever, but it was all she dared to take. Matt had already made it plain that he was a little in love with her and she could very easily reciprocate his feelings. How wonderful it would be if they could allow those budding emotions to flower, but it couldn't be.

Lying on her side with his arm draped over her waist, she allowed her gaze to linger on Matt. She let her eyes lovingly caress every intriguing inch of him, from his dark, tousled chest over the flat planes of his

stomach. Her heart skipped erratically as she recalled
the taste of his skin, the wonders of his touch. She
sighed softly and, after brushing a light kiss across the
corner of his mouth, she slipped from his embrace and
went to take a shower.

The cool water seemed to wash away the last of her
doubts. As much as she wished it could be otherwise,
she had to convince Matt that they should break things
off now, before they got any more complicated. He
thought he knew everything about her, but there was
so much more and when he found out he would be
devastated.

She went back into the bedroom after putting on her
lingerie and a rust-colored tweed wool suit and gold
blouse that usually did spectacular things for her vi-
brant coloring. A glance in the mirror told her that
despite the incredible way she was feeling, today she
looked paler than usual, and the blasted puffiness under her eyes made her look as though she'd been on a
week-long bender. "Hey, sleepyhead," she called out.

"Umm," Matt mumbled groggily. Apparently he
was not at his best in the morning.

"It's time to get up."

He buried his head under the pillow.

"Matt, the house is on fire."

More mumbles.

Meg poised at the edge of the bed and ran her nails
down the bare curve of his spine. It was a dangerous
tactic, she knew. One quick move on his part and she'd
be right back in his arms instead of on her way to
work. Fortunately, quick moves before eight were ap-

parently not Matt's style. He did roll over and scowl at her, though. It was a very sexy scowl for a man who only had one eye open.

"Good morning to you, too," she said dryly as she sat down at her dressing table.

"Wha' time is it?" He sounded like he was talking with a mouthful of gelatin.

"It's seven-thirty."

"In the morning?"

"Last time I checked."

"Why are you up?"

"I have to go to work. Don't you?"

"Not in the middle of the night."

"We just established it was morning."

"Not by my standards. That's why I'm a private investigator. I only function really well after dark."

"In that case maybe I should have gotten you up at six."

"You did," he murmured seductively. "Don't you remember?"

"So," she said, giving him a satisfied look. "Your mind is not quite as woolly as you've been pretending."

One brow rose a fraction of an inch and one green eye peered at her. "Meg Blake, did you trick me?"

"How could I, a mere interior decorator, trick an astute private eye such as yourself?"

He groaned. "You tricked me."

"I needed you awake."

"Oh, really?" His interest definitely seemed to perk up.

"To talk."

"Oh."

"I just wanted to tell you that you don't owe me anything because of last night," she said, catching his reflection in the mirror as she put on her makeup, hoping to add some color before Matt noticed her pallor. He was sprawled across her bed in a pose that was entirely too provocative. The sheet looked as though it had been draped by a photographer for a very explicit woman's magazine. A shiver of excitement raced along her spine. If she kept up this survey, she'd take her new suit right back off. Quickly, she averted her gaze. Concentrating on her eye shadow, she waited for Matt's response. She didn't have to wait long.

"It's a good thing," he retorted, "because I'm a little short on cash this morning."

Her brows shot up and she turned to face him indignantly. "Why you—"

"Gotcha," he said with an audacious grin. "Now stop saying things like that. They won't work anyway."

"What won't work?"

He smothered a yawn. "Trying to get rid of me. I told you before that you're stuck with me, even though I'm too old and tired to keep up with you."

The conversation was not going as she had planned. Matt didn't seem to be taking her seriously. He was supposed to be relieved by her blasé attitude. If she really wanted him out of her life she'd have to explain everything and she couldn't very well do that. She fought an inner battle with her common sense and lost. Common sense could not stand up to a man who made her blood sizzle. She didn't want him to go. Not yet, anyway. A few more days. A week. She deserved that much happiness, didn't she?

"If you don't quit moaning about how old and creaky you are, I might start believing you...despite the evidence to the contrary you displayed last night. If that happens, you'll be having oatmeal and prunes for breakfast, instead of the light, fluffy waffles I had in mind." Her voice was deliberately sultry and provocative, all thoughts of ending their affair abandoned for the moment.

His eyes lit up. "You're going to fix waffles?"

"I thought I might. Interested?"

"I'm more interested in you, but since you have too many clothes on for me to do much about that, I suppose I can make do with waffles."

"Clothes do come off," she taunted.

His eyes brightened and he grinned wickedly. Then his expression sobered. "But you'd be late for work," he said solemnly.

"That's true."

"I wouldn't want to be responsible for that." He sounded very noble. Meg wasn't sure if she should thank him or strangle him.

"You truly do have a martyr complex," she grumbled finally as she walked out of the bedroom. She called back over her shoulder, "I suppose a man your age really is too weak to handle much more excitement anyway."

"Why you sharp-tongued wench!" Matt sprang out of bed as Meg winked at him.

"Breakfast in twenty minutes," she said sweetly, dodging his hand and escaping down the stairs.

Matt was in the kitchen in fifteen so he could watch Meg as she moved efficiently around the cheerful, sunny room, careful to avoid stepping on Ginger, who'd plopped down in the middle of the floor. She moved with the grace of a dancer, her lithe body taunting him even more now that he knew some of the secrets it held. He had a feeling a lifetime wouldn't be long enough to fully discover them all. During the long, extraordinarily satisfying night, the specter of her disease had been hidden beneath a silken haze of passion and ecstasy. Now, in the bright light of day, he knew it was time to bring it out of the shadows again. She had to be reassured that he wouldn't be frightened away. And after years of self-imposed silence, she needed to talk about it. Moreover, he needed to listen if he was to understand something that was such an integral part of a woman with whom he was very rapidly falling in love. Then, perhaps, they could put the subject aside and concentrate on their future together.

The realization of what was happening made his breath catch in his throat. The last thing Matt had expected, when Duncan had sent him after Meg, was to fall in love with her. Hell, after Paula and the body blow she'd delivered to his ability to trust, he'd never expected to fall in love again at all. Yet, it was happening and with a woman whose life was so complex he knew that she wouldn't make loving her an easy thing to do. It was clear from her persistent attempts at withdrawal, no matter how feeble they had been, that she would be terrified by the intensity of his feelings. If he was to overcome the barriers between them, he would have to discover the sad, lonely child she'd been as well as the intelligent, cautious woman she'd become.

"What did you miss most when your parents became so protective and kept you at home so much?"

"Analyzing me?" she inquired with a grin.

"Getting to know you."

"Same difference."

"Does that mean I'm not going to get an answer?"

"Not if I expect to get to work on time this morning. I'm meeting an important client at nine to look at carpeting and wallpaper for an office complex."

"Sounds boring. How about meeting me for lunch?"

"Sorry. Another client."

"Dinner?"

She shrugged. "I don't know what time I'll be free."

"I'll wait."

She studied him closely, then nodded and reached into a kitchen cupboard. She handed him a key. "This time come inside. I don't want to be responsible for your aches and pains."

"You already are," he taunted.

"*Those* you'd better learn to live with. By the way, if I'm late, you can feed Ginger while you're waiting."

The dog wagged her tail appreciatively and draped her head across his foot. Her allegiance and food were clearly tied closely together.

"Do you want me to start dinner?"

"Can you cook?"

"Can I cook?" he repeated indignantly. "Just you wait."

"No meat," she warned.

"Meat is good for you. It builds muscles. You could use a few."

"I don't want any more muscles, thank you. You didn't have any complaints about my body last night."

"Certainly not," he agreed.

"Then stick with salad."

"Rabbit food," he muttered, as he followed her to the door.

"Rabbit food is healthy."

"If you're a rabbit."

She shook her head in exasperation. "Fix what you want."

"Thank you." He swept her into his arms and kissed her resoundingly. When she was breathless and flushed, he released her. "Have a good day," he taunted lightly as he strolled away.

Matt had a very enlightening day. He went to his office, flicked on his answering machine while he shaved and listened to an assortment of increasingly strident messages from disgruntled clients. He called those he had to, then spent the rest of the morning on a new investigation—trying to discover what teenagers did for fun. He intended to return to Meg some of the excitement she'd missed. He might not be able to take her to her senior prom, but he could find other things they could share. Not that teenagers today were anything like they had been when she'd been in high school. They certainly weren't anything like the kids he'd known.

Struck by a sudden inspiration, he picked up the phone and called his sister. "I need to borrow your kids," he said without preamble.

"You can have them," Sally retorted.

"I don't want them to keep."

She gave an exaggerated sigh. "I knew it was too good to be true. What exactly do you want them for?"

"I want them to tell me what they like to do."

"I can tell you that. They like to play the stereo so loud it rattles the windows, they like to eat pizza and potato chips and leave the remains all over the house, they like to go to the movies, especially if they're R-rated and they love video games, but mainly if they're in a shopping mall and cost a fortune in quarters to play. You didn't ask, but I can also add that they rarely do what they're told the first time, they absolutely never, ever clean their rooms and they refuse to wear clothes that don't have a designer label."

Matt's grin widened as Sally raged on. "Did you have a bad morning, sis?"

"Every morning is bad around here. So are the evenings. The only peaceful time is noon and I'm not even here to enjoy it."

"Maybe I ought to talk to my nieces myself. You seem to have a rather jaded outlook."

"My outlook's not jaded. I'm speaking with the voice of experience. I tell you, if you want to understand these kids you should take them home with you for a month."

"That's okay. I think maybe I'll just wing it."

"Wing it? What are you talking about?"

"I'm thinking of going back in time for awhile."

"You're what? Are you on something, Matthew Flanagan?"

"Nope. Just high on life, sis. See you later."

When he hung up, Sally was still sputtering questions at him. It's a good thing he didn't plan to be home tonight. She'd probably be over to take his temperature. She was three years older and had always had a bit of a mothering complex where he was concerned, probably because their own mother had died when they were still in high school—Sally a senior, he a freshman. She'd had a lot of practice before having her own children and, despite her grumblings, he knew she wouldn't trade her family for anything. She'd picked herself up after her divorce and carried on with style and courage. He'd always envied the warm home his sister had made for herself and the girls, but after Paula he'd despaired of ever finding one like it.

Until now. His feelings for Meg held the promise of a future filled with warmth and unexpected thrills. He had a feeling Meg would never be conventional, her response to him wasn't something he could ever take for granted. He already knew that she was an intriguing blend of excitement and caution, of generosity and restraint, of exuberance and sadness. He wanted to banish the caution and sorrow forever. He wanted her to have a chance to live life to its fullest.

He started that night by taking her ice skating.

"Matt, I don't know how to skate," Meg protested as he bundled her straight into his car after ordering her to put on warm slacks and a sweater.

"Neither do I."

"Then why on earth are we going?"

"It'll be fun."

"Not when we're sitting on the ice, freezing our bruised tails off."

He regarded her triumphantly. "Is that what your parents always told you?"

She nodded sagely. "Yes and I think I'm beginning to see."

"See what?"

"Why we're going skating."

"So, then. Are you game?"

Suddenly she laughed, and Matt's heart flipped over. She looked almost like the kid in the photograph. "Why not?" she said, kissing him lightly. "As long as you promise to bring me flowers and milk shakes in the hospital."

"You're not going to get sick."

"Of course not," she said agreeably. "But I may break several of my bones."

"Nope. I'm told this is very soft ice."

"In that case, we probably shouldn't be skating on it."

"Don't be cute."

"By the way, what are we doing about dinner? I spent all day dreaming about this feast you were planning for me."

"It's right here."

She eyed the lumpy package warily. "That's not a salad."

"Nope."

She poked at the paper bag on the seat between them. "What is it then? Chinese carryout? I love Chinese food almost as much as I like salad."

"I'm not surprised, but sorry. It's hot dogs and marshmallows."

"You're kidding." She looked at him closely and groaned. "You're not kidding. Matt, do you know what they put into hot dogs?"

"No." He turned and scowled at her as she started to open her mouth in further protest. "And I don't want to know either."

"It is not good to have a closed mind."

"In certain instances, it is. Hot dogs being one of those instances. One savors hot dogs cooked over an open flame. One does not analyze their nutritional value."

"They have no nutritional value."

"That is not true," he grumbled. "Talk about a closed mind."

Meg groaned. "Okay. Okay. I'll eat a hot dog. I don't suppose it'll kill me."

"And several marshmallows."

"Yes."

"That's better."

Actually, Meg admitted hours later, when she was curled up in Matt's arms in her bed, it was one of the best meals she'd ever had. "But only because I'd nearly starved to death waiting for it. Some camper you turned out to be. Didn't it ever occur to you that it might be difficult to light a fire with wood that's been drenched by rain and snow? Even I would have known enough to bring along kindling or papers."

"I got it started, didn't I?" he growled.

"Finally. Thank goodness you hadn't cleaned those Popsicle sticks out of your jacket pockets," she said sweetly. "How does a grown man accumulate so many of those?"

"I happen to like grape Popsicles. They help me think."

"I thought maybe you just liked to collect the sticks."

"No," he retorted solemnly. "I only collect ashtrays. The prize in my collection is from the men's room at the Waldorf-Astoria."

"Now that you've stopped smoking do you plan to give up this rather unusual hobby?"

"I hadn't thought about it. Maybe I should start picking up silverware. I was in a really fancy restaurant just the other night . . ."

"Matt!"

He grinned at her. "Okay. Forget that. I'll stick to ashtrays."

"I'd rather you abandoned all of your light-fingered tendencies. I'd hate to have to bail you out of the slammer some night over an ashtray."

"Have you ever bailed anybody out of jail before?"

She shook her head.

"See. Then it will be an experience."

"I think I'd rather have you drag me skating again."

"After your fifth fall, you told me you wouldn't go skating again until hell froze over."

"I think the ice has started forming."

"Terrific. We'll go again tomorrow."

"Wait a minute. I wouldn't want to overdo it."

"Okay," Matt said agreeably. "You choose. What would you like to do for your next adventure?"

She eyed him skeptically. "I can pick anything I want?"

"Absolutely."

She pursed her lips thoughtfully, then finally her eyes lit up and she gave him a wicked grin. "I'd like to have a slumber party."

"A slumber party?" Matt repeated weakly. "You mean with a bunch of people?"

"Exactly. With popcorn and pizza and the stereo up and boys sneaking in. I always thought that would be such fun," she said wistfully.

"Oh, my Lord."

"You said I could have anything."

"So I did." His expression brightened. "I don't suppose you'd settle for staying up all night with me."

She shook her head. "It wouldn't be the same."

"I thought it might be better," he huffed indignantly.

"Don't go getting your masculine feathers all ruffled, Flanagan. I'll stay up all night with you another night."

He studied her closely, a soft light coming into his eyes. "This is really important to you, isn't it?"

Meg hesitated, then returned his gaze. "It started out as a joke," she admitted slowly, "But, yes, I think it is important. I never had girlfriends over for the night and I never went to anyone else's house. My parents were afraid I'd have a reaction or something and pass out."

Matt tightened his arms around her and kissed her gently. "Okay, babe. I'll work on it."

Right before they fell asleep, Matt was struck by a sense of panic. Where the hell was he supposed to find a bunch of girls to attend a slumber party for a twenty-seven-year-old woman?

Six

The next few days passed in an absolute whirlwind of unexpected delights. Matt was gentle, attentive and wildly determined to please Meg. He turned up at every hour of the day and night, always ready with something to lure Meg away from what she was doing. It was playing havoc with her routine, but it was absolutely thrilling her senses.

"Come on," he said one evening, his eyes sparkling with mischievousness as he twirled her swivel chair around and tugged her to her feet.

Laughing, Meg tried to resist. "Matt, I have work to do."

"You work too hard."

"And you don't seem to work at all."

"Oh, I get the job done. Right now I have more important things on my mind."

"Such as?"

"Such as getting you out of this stuffy old office and into a bowling alley."

"A bowling alley? You've got to be kidding."

"I never kid about bowling. Next to making coffee, bowling is what I do best."

"I thought making love was what you did best."

"Thank you."

"You're welcome."

"Now put your coat on and stop stalling."

"Matt, I've never bowled."

"A sophisticated lady like you should try everything at least once."

An hour later Meg wondered if he was regretting his determination. He seemed doggedly cheerful, no matter how disastrous her attempts were, but his smile seemed to be growing just a little weaker with each passing minute.

"Meg, we're playing on *this* alley."

"I know that. Do you think I meant to roll the ball down there?"

"No, but I'm sure that man appreciated your knocking down the rest of his pins."

"At least the ball went forward that time."

"Actually it went sideways, but I'm sure the players in the next lane appreciated the improvement. They told me they'd never had a bowling ball knock over a whole tray of beers before."

"This was your idea."

"And it was a good idea. Admit it. You're having fun."

"Actually I am, but you seem a little less enthusiastic than you were when you came into my office."

"I could use another beer."

The next day at noon he turned up with a bouquet of violets and her tennis shoes.

"Okay, I'll bite. What's up now? Where did you find violets at this time of the year?"

"Don't even ask," he muttered. "Let's go."

"Go where? I have a business lunch."

"No, you don't. Your secretary rescheduled the meeting for three o'clock."

"She what? Marjorie, get in here right this minute!" Meg bellowed.

"She can't hear you. I sent her to lunch so you couldn't yell at her."

Meg leaned back in her chair and moaned. "You are the pushiest, most irritating man I have ever known."

"We don't have time to debate my merits, love. If we don't get moving, you'll be late for your three o'clock appointment."

"Where are we going? Please don't tell me we're going bowling again."

"Nope. I thought we'd try a bike ride along the Potomac."

"Matt, are you crazy? I can't go biking in this suit."

"Of course you can't. Your jogging suit is right outside. I'll get it."

"Coward. Did you figure I'd wrap it around your neck, if you brought it in?"

"Let's just say I thought maybe the violets would help put you in a good mood and the tennis shoes would begin to ease you into the idea." He regarded her hopefully. "Did it work?"

"It worked."

On another afternoon they went sightseeing and on yet another they went to a theater matinee. At night they made blissful love until Meg knew a contentment greater than anything she could ever have imagined.

Still, there were shadows. She knew that things could not go on like this indefinitely. She felt a little like Cinderella watching the clock tick away the minutes before midnight. Her growing exhaustion reminded her that she couldn't delay breaking this relationship off much longer, not with Matt becoming more and more deeply involved. Although he hadn't said that he loved her, his love was in everything he did. She deluded herself that if she said goodbye before he actually spoke the words aloud, neither his pain nor her guilt would be so great.

With an uncommon selfishness, though, she hadn't been able to make herself do it. Only one more day, she told herself over and over, and at the end of each day she'd gone into his arms and held on, thrilling in the magic of his touch. In the morning the words just wouldn't come.

She was sitting at her desk on Friday, her lips curved into a soft smile as she recalled Matt's tenderness, when the door of her office slammed against the wall and Matt stalked in, his eyes glittering fiercely. She recognized the stance. It was the posture he always assumed when he was feeling particularly protective and possessive. He'd been adopting it more and more the last couple of days as he noted the signs of exhaustion she'd no longer been able to hide. He'd grumbled at her for wearing herself out, ignoring her dry retorts that he was at least partially responsible.

"Where have you been?" he growled.

She reacted instinctively to his harsh tone, drawing into herself and staring back at him coolly. All of the warm thoughts she'd been having vanished. She hated his occasional lord-of-the-manor moods, no matter how well intentioned.

"I beg your pardon," she said stiffly.

"I asked where the hell you've been."

"Working."

"You weren't here at ten."

She hesitated. "I was with a client."

"Not according to your calendar. Your secretary checked for me."

"Since when do you have the right to check up on me?"

"I wasn't checking up."

Suddenly he sighed and collapsed into the chair across from her. He gave her what for him was an apologetic smile. "Okay," he admitted ruefully. "I was checking up. I'm sorry, Meg. I was worried about you."

She stared at him blankly. "Why?"

"I thought...hell, I don't know what I thought. It's just that you look so damned tired, and it's not the first time this week I've tried to find you and no one seems to know where you've gone.''

"Am I supposed to give you a daily schedule and call in with updates?''

"You could at least leave word with your secretary. What if something important came up?''

"Do you have some objection to the way I run my business now, too?''

"No, of course not, but—''

"But nothing. I am perfectly capable of running my own career, Matt. As you perfectly well know since you're *never* in your office, sometimes things come up at the last minute. They are not always on my calendar.''

"Okay. You're right. Don't make such a big deal out of it.''

"You were the one making a big deal out of it.'' She regarded him curiously. "What are you really upset about?'' Suddenly it dawned on her and she didn't like it very much. "You thought I had an insulin reaction or something, didn't you?''

He returned her gaze sheepishly. "I guess so. My imagination jumped into overdrive again.''

Meg got up and went to kneel by him. She put her hands on his thighs and stared into his eyes. Now was the time.

She took a deep breath, then blurted, "Matt, the last few days have been incredible, but I think it's time we stopped seeing each other.''

"What! Just because I got a little worried?''

...be tempted!

See inside for special
4 FREE BOOKS offer

 Silhouette Desire™

Discover deliciously different romance with 4 Free Novels from

Silhouette Desire ™

Sit back and enjoy four exciting romances—yours **FREE** from Silhouette Books! But wait . . . there's *even more* to this great offer! You'll also get . . .

A COMPACT MANICURE SET—ABSOLUTELY FREE! You'll love your beautiful manicure set—an elegant and useful accessory to carry in your handbag. Its rich burgundy case is a perfect expression of your style and good taste—and it's yours free with this offer!

PLUS A FREE MYSTERY GIFT—A surprise bonus that will delight you!

You can get all this just for trying Silhouette Desire!

MONEY-SAVING HOME DELIVERY!

Once you receive your 4 FREE books and gifts, you'll be able to preview more great romance reading in the convenience of your own home at less than retail prices. Every month we'll deliver 6 brand-new Silhouette Desire novels right to your door months before they appear in stores. If you decide to keep them, they'll be yours for only $2.24 each! That's 26¢ less per book than what you pay in stores—with no additional charges for home delivery!

SPECIAL EXTRAS—FREE!

You'll also get our monthly newsletter, packed with news of your favorite authors and upcoming books—FREE! And as a valued reader, we'll be sending you additional free gifts from time to time—as a token of our appreciation.

BE TEMPTED! COMPLETE, DETACH AND MAIL YOUR POSTPAID ORDER CARD TODAY AND RECEIVE 4 FREE BOOKS, A MANICURE SET AND A MYSTERY GIFT—PLUS LOTS MORE!

A FREE
Manicure Set
and Mystery Gift *await you, too!*

(keep this and the opposite card, mail)

Silhouette Desire™

Silhouette Books
901 Fuhrmann Blvd., P.O. Box 9013, Buffalo, NY 14240-9963

☐ **YES!** Please rush me my four Silhouette Desire novels with my FREE Manicure Set and Mystery Gift, as explained on the opposite page. I understand that I am under no obligation to purchase any books. The free books and gifts remain mine to keep.

225 CIY JAX8

NAME _____
(please print)

ADDRESS _____ APT. _____

CITY _____ STATE _____ ZIP _____

Offer limited to one per household and not valid for present subscribers.
Prices subject to change.

PRINTED IN U.S.A.

She pressed her fingers to his lips to silence him. "Wait, love. Listen to me. It's no good if you're going to start treating me like a fragile doll. That's exactly what my parents did. I won't allow it. It just makes me feel more out of control than ever."

Matt ran his fingers gently along her cheek, then captured a handful of her hair. It felt like silk and it smelled, he knew, like fresh air and spring flowers. It was a scent that did the strangest things to his pulse which was now skittering like a nervous teenager's.

"I know that and, believe me, I don't want to worry. I want you to live your life to the fullest, but for just a minute this morning I panicked. I promise it won't happen again."

"Oh, Matt," she murmured and rested her head on his knee. "It will happen again and you know it. That's the kind of man you are. Let me go now before we ruin what we have with a lot of anger and resentment."

His fingers curved under her chin and gently forced her head up until she was returning his gaze. "Don't ask that of me, Meg. I can't do it. I can't let you go and I certainly can't leave you." The thought of losing her terrified him. He had no idea how she had become so important in such a short time. He only knew that she had found a niche in his heart and filled it with her wit, her vulnerability and the joy she seemed to grasp for so desperately in each moment. He rejoiced in the sound of her laughter.

"I will try to stop hovering over you, though," he promised.

Her expression wavered between relief and dismay. Once more she'd tried to break it off, but hadn't been able to make it stick. Her resolve was growing weaker with each passing day, and she wondered when she'd turned into such a coward. Finally she admitted with a tiny smile, "I don't mind if you worry just a little. It means you care."

"Oh, I care all right." He moaned, pulling her onto his lap. His lips captured hers hungrily. There was an urgency about the kiss that sent a shudder straight through Meg. He felt it and wanted desperately to lock the door of her office and make love to her right then and there, just to prove to himself that she was okay and that she was truly his.

Instead, he drew back and ran a finger lightly across her lips, which were still swollen and tender from his kiss. His finger trembled.

"Feel better?" she asked, her blue eyes shining up at him. The look in those eyes made him feel ten feet tall.

"Not exactly," he mumbled, shifting awkwardly in the chair. "You don't exactly have a calming influence on me."

She grinned at his obvious discomfort. "Oh, really?" she said innocently. "Want me to get up?"

"In a week or so."

"Why'd you call earlier?" she asked, nibbling on his ear. He groaned. "Am I bothering you?"

"You know perfectly well you are," he said, shifting again beneath her. "Behave yourself," he warned.

"Spoilsport," she grumbled. "Now tell me why you were looking for me."

"I just wanted to let you know I'd pick you up at seven to go to my sister's."

Meg's heart fluttered. She wasn't at all sure she was ready to meet his family. He'd told her a lot about Sally and his nieces. It was clear he was very fond of them and that they'd drawn even closer together since Sally's breakup with her husband. What would they think of her when she left Matt? They'd hate her for hurting him, and she wouldn't blame them. It would be better if they all never met.

Still, she consoled herself, Matt had been adamant about tonight and, to be perfectly truthful, she was looking forward to seeing another side of him. For all of his possessiveness, in the end he was as stubbornly independent as she was. It would be a revelation to see how he interacted with his family.

"Should I dress up?"

"No, I think jeans would be in order. It's going to be a casual evening. Don't forget to take your insulin along in case we're late." He kissed her again. "See you later."

As Meg watched him go, she hugged his words to her. Despite his earlier overreaction to her absence, Matt really had made every effort to accept her diabetes. He didn't try to pretend it didn't exist. When he mentioned it, as he had just now, it was as casually as he might have reminded someone else to take along an aspirin for a cold.

Initially he'd asked dozens of questions about the machine that tested her blood sugar level, about signs he should know that would indicate that she was having a problem. He'd given her one of her injections. One night he'd turned up with a stack of books from the library and had bombarded her with new questions as he read them all. He'd refused to let her hide any aspect of the disease from him. She was grateful for his matter-of-fact attitude except for one thing: it made her love him all the more.

When Matt arrived that night, she was wearing a heavy hand-knit sweater, jeans and boots. She had her coat by the door. He gave her a quick, distracted kiss, then brushed past her.

"I'll be right back," he said, taking the stairs two at a time. Ginger, who'd become almost as big a fan of Matt as Meg had, lumbered up the steps behind him, then regarded him accusingly when he dashed back down.

"Are you okay?" Meg asked, her gaze troubled.

"Sure. I just needed to get something."

Meg shrugged and put on her coat. Despite the forlorn tilt of Ginger's head, they left to make the drive into Virginia to Sally's. A half hour later they were pulling up in front of a small town house in an area of Alexandria that was being revitalized. The porch light beamed a welcome and a cat sat perched in a window. It jumped to the floor as Matt rang the bell.

Meg could hear a chorus of excited giggles from behind the door just before it was thrown open by a woman whose hair was the same rich brown shade as

Matt's and just as casually styled. Her hazel eyes sparkled at Meg and she held out her hands.

"You must be Meg," she said in a musical voice that was as low and as soothing as a ballad. "Welcome to bedlam. The girls wanted to have everything just so for you, but organization has never been one of their strong points. They're working on it, though. Aren't you girls?"

"It's not that bad, Mom. We're almost finished," the older girl, Marcie, said, throwing her arms around Matt and planting a kiss on his cheek. He seemed embarrassed and pleased. "Hi, Uncle Matt. It's about time you brought one of your women over for us to inspect."

Meg lifted an eyebrow and muttered, "One of your women?"

Matt choked. "The girls exaggerate," he protested weakly.

"No, we don't," Carrie, a blond pixie, countered, facing him rebelliously. "When Mom asks you about your love life, you always tell her you've got a different woman for every night of the week."

"Gee, what have they been doing for the last week?" Meg asked far too pleasantly. He sensed he had not heard the last of this. "They must be getting lonely."

"That's true," Sally agreed cheerfully. "Maybe you can get caught up with your Friday night regular tonight, while Meg's here with us."

"That's enough," Matt roared as Sally barely managed to smother her laughter.

She grinned at Meg and took her arm. "Let's go into the living room and see what Matt and the girls have cooked up for you."

"For me?"

"Don't ask questions. Just come along," Matt insisted, looking like an excited kid on Christmas morning.

They walked through an archway and Meg drew to a stop, her eyes widening, then filling with tears. There were four sleeping bags rolled up in a corner. There was a stack of videotapes by the cassette player. Bowls of popcorn were sitting on the coffee table.

"We've ordered pizza," Carrie announced importantly. "With everything. Uncle Matt wasn't sure how you like it."

"You remembered," she breathed softly, her eyes riveted to Matt's.

"Of course, I remembered. It won't be a very big slumber party, though. Just Carrie, Marcie, Sally and me..."

His comment was met with giggles.

"You can't stay, Uncle Matt," Marcie protested.

"What do you mean I can't stay? I planned this party."

"Boys can't stay," Marcie insisted.

"That's right," Sally agreed. "It wouldn't be proper. Now you run along, Matthew."

"Run along," he sputtered. "I will not. Where Meg sleeps, I..." His voice trailed off as the girls stared up at him expectantly. "Never mind."

"I knew you'd catch on," Sally said, beaming her approval. "Feel free to come back for breakfast."

"Hell," he grumbled. Meg followed him to the door, then stood on tiptoe and kissed him, a long, leisurely kiss that sent waves of warmth cascading through him. Reluctantly, he pulled away. "That's enough of that if you expect me to leave you alone here."

"I won't be alone," Meg said brightly.

"No," he agreed. "I will. I'm beginning to think this was a rotten idea."

"No, it wasn't. It was a wonderful idea." She nuzzled against him. "Matt, how can I ever thank you?"

"Just have a good time." He grinned at her. "And get this slumber party stuff out of your system. I don't intend to let you sleep apart from me again."

"Who said anything about sleeping?"

"It is a slumber party, isn't it?"

"Sure. But you don't sleep. That's the whole point."

"Women," he muttered in disgust. "I had no idea female perversity started at such a young age. Do you realize my nieces already think like you do?"

"I like them very much."

"Good, because you're going to be around them a lot. Now go on back in there and party the night away."

Suddenly Meg's face fell. "Oh, no. I don't have a toothbrush or anything."

"Whoops! Yes, you do," Matt said, reaching into his pockets. He pulled out her toothbrush and toothpaste. "You did remember your insulin?"

She feigned a ferocious scowl. "Matthew!"

"Sorry."

She regarded him hopefully. "I don't suppose you thought to tuck a nightgown in your pocket, too?"

"Nope."

"Oh, dear."

"But I think you'll find one that's just your size in with the sleeping bags. It has the cutest little bears on it. I thought about getting one of those pajama things with feet, but decided you might want to wear it when you're with me."

"Matt, you are the sweetest man."

He brushed a kiss across her forehead. "Don't let it get around. It'll ruin my reputation."

"My lips are sealed. If you think I want the competition to know about this, you're crazy."

"Good night, love."

"Good night." Meg watched as he started down the steps, then called him back. "Matt, would you kiss me again?"

He grinned at her and ran back up the steps. "With pleasure."

Matt's mouth came down lightly on hers, his lips as soft and gentle as the delicate touch of a butterfly. Meg's heart lurched, then thundered against her ribs as she clung to him, slipping her arms under his jacket so she could feel his solid warmth. He was so dear, so incredibly special, his romantic thoughtfulness so at odds with his rugged exterior and tough profession.

"Uhh, excuse me."

The quivering voice brought them apart and they gazed into the embarrassed eyes of a teenager laden down with boxes of pizza.

Meg's eyes lit up. "I'll take it," she said, her attention immediately shifting from Matt.

He chuckled as he pulled out his wallet and paid the boy. "Don't ever trust a woman who'll abandon you at the first sniff of a pizza," he warned the grinning teen as the youth loped back to his delivery truck.

Matt turned his gaze back to Meg hopefully. "It smells great."

"Doesn't it? We'll save you some."

"I can't come back?" he said, regarding her pitifully.

"No. You're going to have to go and get your own dinner."

"You're a hard woman."

"I thought you knew that when you met up with me. Duncan Blake wouldn't put up with a sissy in the family." She winked and ran back inside. Matt stood on the sidewalk and watched her go with a lump in his throat.

"You're one hell of a woman, Meg Blake, and one of these days soon I'm going to tell you exactly how much I love you," he whispered before he walked away, wondering what the devil he was supposed to do with himself until morning. In just a week he'd gotten accustomed to sharing Meg's bed. The prospect of sleeping alone again made him feel more than a little lost.

Inside the house, Meg, Sally and the girls were already devouring the pizza and watching a videotape of a popular horror movie. To Meg's astonishment, she felt thoroughly at ease with these strangers, possibly because they didn't seem like strangers at all. She already knew that Marcie hated her braces and was crazy about boys. Carrie was a tomboy and was furious because she couldn't play on her school's softball team. And ever since her husband had left, Sally had worked as a real estate agent to support her family. Matt had told her all of those things and more. Now Sally was filling in the gaps.

"I wanted the divorce," she told Meg. "Even though I knew it was going to be difficult and lonely, I figured it was bound to be better than living with a man who didn't love me. Larry sees the girls and pays child support, but I didn't ask for alimony."

"You didn't?" Meg was startled.

"It must be my stubborn Irish pride. I wanted to earn my own way. There have been months when I've cursed myself for being a fool, but in the end I think it was the right thing to do. I like knowing that this place belongs to me."

"To us," Marcie corrected, and Sally chuckled.

"That's right. The girls chip in baby-sitting money every now and then, when the real estate market is tight."

"You must be very proud of them."

"I am," Sally said easily, "even when I grumble because they don't clean up their rooms or do their homework." She glowered at them pointedly. Marcie stuck out her tongue, and Carrie groaned.

Sally shrugged. "You see how much respect I get." She regarded Meg expectantly. "Enough about us. Now tell me about you and Matt. The girls and I are dying of curiosity."

"There's not much to tell."

"Don't give me that. Like Marcie said earlier, Matt has never brought another woman over here. You must be very special to him."

"We've only known each other for a week."

"It's amazing how much you can learn about another person in a week. Are you in love with him?"

Meg looked away, gazing forlornly into the fire as she pondered her reply. Sally saved her from having to answer.

"I'm sorry. I'm pushing. Matt would kill me. It's just that we all so want to see him happy."

"I want that, too," Meg said. "More that anything."

The mood had gotten far too somber for a slumber party. Meg forced a smile and glanced at Marcie and Carrie. "Okay. That's enough girl talk for awhile. What do we do now?"

"Do you want to play charades?"

"Sounds like fun."

They played charades, watched a horror movie and played several albums while the girls taught Sally and her the latest dance steps. Every time one of them started to drift asleep, it was Meg who nudged them awake again. By dawn they were all giggling from lack of sleep and everyone except Meg was stuffed with junk food. She'd sampled everything, but been cautious to monitor her intake. If anyone had noticed, they hadn't said anything.

When they heard the paper thump on the sidewalk outside, it was Meg who went to get it as the girls settled down in their sleeping bags. She found Matt on the doorstep, half-asleep. She dropped down beside him.

"Morning," she whispered and kissed his ear.

"Trying to turn the sleeping frog into a prince?"

"You're already a prince in my book."

"Is breakfast ready?"

"Actually, I think you're going to have to forget about breakfast. The girls just fell asleep on the floor and when I came out here, Sally said something about dragging herself upstairs to take a bath."

"A fine lot you are. I've been up half the night anticipating this breakfast, and you're casting me out into the world unfed."

"I doubt you'll starve, but come inside and I'll warm up some pizza."

"Ugh!"

"Popcorn?"

He wrinkled his nose. "I'll take you out for pancakes, eggs and sausage."

Meg moaned. "No more. Have pity on a poor woman who's been eating for the last twelve hours straight."

"Then you can watch me eat."

She grinned at him. "I'll watch you anytime."

"Then put on your clothes and let's get moving, woman. I want to eat, then get home and get some sleep."

"You haven't slept either?"

"I couldn't sleep without you," he admitted sheepishly. "Now scat. Get dressed."

"We ought to wait for Sally. I should thank her for everything."

"Write her a note."

Meg left a note for Sally on top of the television, then joined Matt in the car. He drove a few blocks to an all-night restaurant so he could get his breakfast. As they were walking inside, Meg felt a little weak, and as she was telling Matt all about the slumber party, she felt her body growing cold and clammy. She recognized the symptoms, but tried to convince herself she was wrong. Then, suddenly she was trembling and she knew she was in trouble.

"Matt!"

He looked up from his plate, and Meg saw his eyes widen with dismay. She wanted to tell him something, but she couldn't get the words out. She was far too shaky and she couldn't seem to think clearly.

"Meg?" Matt's voice was filled with urgency and it seemed to be coming from very far away.

"Matt, I feel funny," she mumbled.

She felt his hand grab hers and hold on tightly. "Meg?" he repeated. "What is it? Tell me exactly how you feel."

"Strange. Like I'm very far away and I'm so cold."
She shivered uncontrollably.

And then, before Matt could do a thing to help her,
her world went dark.

Seven

When Meg came to, she was in an emergency room, hooked up to an IV, a thin blanket tucked around her. The room reeked of antiseptic and even though the door was closed, it was filled with the eerie sounds of beeping machines and moaning patients. A shudder ran through her. Her eyes swept the room seeking reassurance.

A pale and disheveled Matt was slumped into a chair next to her stretcher, his eyes closed. His fingers were curled tightly around hers.

"Oh, damn," she muttered, fighting tears while struggling to come fully awake. Why had this had to happen? She'd never wanted Matt to see her like this, never wanted him to be a witness to her helplessness. She hadn't had a hypoglycemic reaction in years, not since the first months of the disease, when she'd been rebelling against the constraints it placed on her life and hadn't been eating properly. Passing out a few times had scared the daylights out of her and more than anything else that had finally convinced her she'd better listen to the doctor.

This time the fainting spell must have been brought on by lack of sleep and the extra exercise—the dancing that had been so much fun at the time—plus the stress of meeting Matt's family. She'd been so careful to try to balance her food and insulin intake, but apparently her calculations had been off. She should have snacked more during the long, active night.

Once more the blasted diabetes had won, she thought miserably.

Matt shifted uncomfortably in his chair, then opened his eyes. When he saw that she was awake, his lips curved into a smile, but his eyes were filled with concern.

"Hi," he said softly, standing up and leaning over to run a finger along her cheek. A shiver raced through her. Meg captured his hand and held it in place, his palm slightly rough and very warm against her skin. Matt's hands were so strong, yet so tender, and she felt such incredible spirals of pleasure just from that simple touch.

"How do you feel?"

"Better. I don't suppose it was the flu or something?" she asked hopefully.

Matt grinned at her. "Nice try, but no. The doctor said you probably overdid it a bit. I'm sorry."

"What on earth are you sorry about?"

"The slumber party was my idea and, on top of that, I forgot to warn Sally or to bring along that stuff you told me to give you if you ever started acting weird and passed out."

"No," Meg said adamantly. "You can't take responsibility for my life. I wanted that slumber party and I can't begin to tell you how much fun I had. Thank you for planning it for me."

"It wasn't just the slumber party. It was everything. I've been pushing you too hard, trying to make up for things. I should have seen it was too much for you. You even said so yourself, but I didn't listen. I was so hell-bent on making you happy, I landed you in the hospital instead."

"That's ridiculous. I'm a grown woman, Matt. I didn't do anything I didn't want to do. And speaking of the hospital, when can I go home?"

"You just got here. You haven't even tried the food."

"Matt!"

"The doctor will be back in a minute to check you out and then he'll decide."

"I don't want to stay here. All these tubes and things give me the creeps."

"You'll do whatever the doctor thinks best."

Meg glowered rebelliously at his adamant tone and looked away. Finally she gazed back at him and asked, "Matt, will you do something else for me?"

"Anything."

"When Dr. Mitchell comes back, I want you to go. He'll get someone to take me home."

He shook his head. "No way, babe. I'm staying with you."

"Please, Matt. You just promised."

"Forget it," he said, his lips setting in a stubborn line.

Before Meg could rally a good argument, Dr. Mitchell entered the room, his expression sober. "Well, young lady, it's good to see you awake again."

"Sorry to drag you out on the weekend."

"Don't be silly. You're much prettier than those old goats I play golf with on Saturdays. Now let's take a look at you. Young man, would you leave us alone? Go get yourself a cup of coffee."

Matt scowled at the doctor distrustfully. "I'd rather stay."

The physician smiled at Matt's protectiveness, but remained firm. "Not while I'm examining my patient. You can come back in a few minutes. If you won't go for coffee, then just wait outside the door. I promise I won't try to steal her away from you." He winked at Meg and added, "Though I'd sure like to." She gave him a tremulous smile, then squeezed Matt's hand.

"Matt, please," she urged softly. "Do what he says."

"Okay. Fine," he finally agreed reluctantly. "But I'll be waiting right outside."

When he'd gone, Meg regarded the doctor closely. "What have you told him?"

"Not a thing, other than the obvious."

"Leave it at that. Don't tell him anything else."

"Meg, he was frantic when he brought you in here. It's evident that he cares very deeply about you. Don't you want to talk this out with him?"

"No, and I want to remind you that when this first came up, you promised to maintain my confidentiality. I suspect you've already spilled the beans to my grandfather."

He glowered at her indignantly. "I most certainly did not. Duncan asked a few sly questions, and I evaded them as best I could without telling him an outright lie. You don't need to lecture me about a patient's privacy, young lady.

"But as your friend as well as your doctor, I think it's time you face up to this," he added sternly.

"I am facing up to it in the only way I know how. Matt is not to know, Dr. Mitchell. I couldn't bear it if it changed his feelings toward me."

The doctor sighed and patted Meg's hand. "I've known you since you were a baby, my dear, and if that's the way you want it, I'll abide by your wishes. I just hope you know what you're doing."

A tear slid down Meg's cheek and she brushed it away furiously. She was not going to start crying now. She might never stop. "I hope so, too."

An hour later, Matt was driving Meg home, trying not to hound her with questions. No matter how hard he'd pushed, the damn doctor had refused to tell him a single thing, and Meg was no more help. She'd simply told him she'd been released and asked him to take her home. She'd sat silently beside him all the way. Now that they were pulling up in front of her house, he intended to take her inside, get her settled in front of a nice fire and get some straight answers.

But before he could even switch off the ignition, Meg said, "Thank you for everything you did this morning, Matt, but I don't think you should come in now. I need to get some rest."

Her prim, polite tone set his teeth on edge, and Matt felt his barely restrained temper flare. "Dammit, Meg, don't start treating me like a stranger," he snapped in frustration. "I want to help you."

"Then go home," she said flatly. Matt felt as if a cold knife twisted inside him. If he couldn't tear down this wall she'd begun building when she'd awakened in the hospital, he was going to lose her. But he had no idea how to reach her. He could deal with her fury, could match her shout for shout, but this cool formality was beyond his experience. It scared him.

"I'll call you later," she promised, but the words sounded empty. What he needed was to be there for her, to hold her and care for her. For the first time he sensed some of the despair her parents must have felt, wanting to protect their child only to lose her because of those actions. He knew he should let it rest, but, desperate for answers, he tried again.

"Meg, there's something you're not telling me, isn't there? Today wasn't just a simple reaction. It was something more serious."

Refusing to meet his challenging gaze, she shivered and hugged her arms tightly around her middle. She looked like a child trying to ward off an expected blow. Guilt sped through him. He sighed wearily.

"Okay, forget it for now," he relented. "I'll go. But I'm coming back tomorrow, and we're going to talk."

"If that's what you want," she said without enthusiasm and got out of the car. She didn't even wait for him to walk her to the door.

Matt stayed outside in the car after she'd gone, wondering what the hell was going on. When had her attitude toward him changed? Or was it really different? Maybe he was only just now recognizing a distance between them that had been there all along, a distance he hadn't wanted to acknowledge. He refused to believe that Meg didn't care for him, but something that today's incident had magnified was holding her back.

If he really thought about it, there had been dozens of hints from the very beginning that all was not right with Meg: her desperately carefree life-style, her reluctance to become involved, her mysterious absences, today's attack. All these were evidence of a deeply troubled woman, not just a woman with a manageable disease. Her grandfather had an idea about whatever it was and had been worried enough to call for Matt's help. Now that Matt was in the middle of it, why wouldn't Meg give him all the facts?

Well, apparently Meg hadn't counted on two things—Matt loved her and he was very good at unraveling mysteries. He turned the key in the ignition with an angry gesture and tore out of the parking space. If Meg wouldn't talk, there were other ways to get answers.

He started with Duncan Blake.

"I know about the diabetes," he said, when the old man had given him a drink. Matt took the pack of cigarettes out of his pocket and turned it idly in his hands. For once he wasn't tempted to break down and smoke, but he needed something to do. The cigarettes were an improvement over throwing things.

Duncan sat down across from him and stretched out his legs. His posture was relaxed, but his demeanor was not. He was as skittish as a new colt, his fingers drumming on the arm of the chair.

"Figured you might," he said at last.

"Why didn't you just tell me?"

"It's Meg's business."

"But that is why you wanted me to find her, isn't it? You were worried that she wasn't taking care of herself."

"Something like that," Duncan said vaguely.

"Then there is more?"

"I'm not sure. Ask her."

"Dammit, sir, I'm asking you."

"Son, Meg's an adult. She's got her own way of handling things. I may not approve of all of them, but I'm not going to interfere."

Matt muttered a violent oath under his breath, then pointed out, "You were willing enough to interfere a couple of weeks ago, when you asked me to find her."

"You've done that now."

"And that's all you wanted? I don't buy that. It's not your style."

His direct challenge caused Duncan to stir uncomfortably, just as he'd wanted it to. Duncan was, above all, a fair man, and he adored Meg. Matt used that in his effort to pry some information loose.

"I love her, sir," he added persuasively. "Don't you think I have a right to know?"

Duncan met his gaze evenly. "As a matter of fact, I do. I think you and Meg ought to talk things through. I have my suspicions. I know she's sick, but she won't tell me the complete story."

Damn. Everyone, including Dr. Mitchell, kept telling him to *talk* to Meg. But Meg wasn't talking. Duncan was still his best hope. He decided to use the last of his ammunition.

"She had a severe reaction today that landed her in the hospital," Matt informed the old man coldly. "Do you still think you and I should be sitting around chatting?"

"She what? How is she?" Duncan's voice shook and his hands trembled. He looked every bit his age again as his frantic eyes met Matt's.

"She's at home now, resting," he replied, softening the edge in his voice. "As for the rest, I don't know how the hell she is. She won't tell me. Of course, the doctor won't tell me, and now you've clammed up as though it were a classified military maneuver."

Anxiety and frustration were evident when he pleaded with Duncan, "How can I help her if I don't know what's going on?"

But though Duncan clearly sympathized with him, he held firm.

"I will talk to her, son. Maybe I can get her to open up to both of us. If not, just be there for her. If you care about her as much as you say, you'll do that."

"Oh, I'll stay, sir. I'm going to stick to her like glue."

Whatever attempts Duncan made to get Meg to open up were unsuccessful. When Matt's Sunday visit was equally unproductive, he was forced to resort to other means for finding out what he wanted to know. He decided to begin following her, knowing that if she ever found out, she would be absolutely furious.

On Monday morning, he was sitting in a café across the street from her office when she came out and jumped into a cab. Moving swiftly, he caught another taxi and told the driver to stay with her. She went to a small office building about a mile away. Dashing inside, she reached an elevator ahead of him and disappeared. He watched as it climbed, noting the floors on which it stopped. Then he took the next elevator up and got off on each floor to check the directory, hoping that something would strike a familiar chord. If she was going to see a client she'd never mentioned, he'd lose her, but this was the best he could do. He sure as hell couldn't have ridden the same elevator.

Luck was with him. Grant Mitchell, M.D., was located on the fifth floor. Bingo, he thought, congratulating himself. He opened the office door a crack and saw her sitting in the waiting room, a magazine lying open on her lap. She was staring at the wall. So, he thought, apparently she's come in for a checkup.

She was inside for nearly an hour while Matt paced impatiently in the hallway. When she emerged, he ducked into the stairwell and waited until she'd caught the elevator down before following her again, this time from one furniture store to another for the rest of the afternoon. If it hadn't been Meg he was following, he'd have been bored to tears.

That evening he stopped by her office to pick her up. As he approached her door, he heard her on the phone.

"I have a figure in mind, but I'd like you to make me an offer first. Whatever you think it's worth. My client list has grown considerably in the last year."

Matt listened with a puzzled expression on his face, then walked in. Meg looked up at him, her expression startled and more than a little guilty.

"I have to go now, Robert. Something's come up. Just get back to me by the end of the week, if you can. I'd like to finalize this." She chuckled at something the man said, but there was no laughter in her eyes. "Okay. I'll talk to you soon."

"What was that all about?" Matt asked casually, when she'd hung up.

"Just a business deal."

"It sounded like you might be selling something."

"Playing detective on me, Flanagan?"

"Just curious."

She gave him one of her most dazzling smiles, but it seemed forced. "I'll tell you all about it if it works out," she said brightly and began gathering her things. She refused to meet Matt's gaze. "Let's get out of here. I'm exhausted."

She was out the door before Matt could say another word. He filed the conversation away in the back of his mind. That night after dinner he asked her about her day.

"I picked out the sofa for one of my clients and found half a dozen possible lamps for another one. I'm beginning to think she'll only be satisfied if I find her one with a genie inside."

She was sitting on the sofa with her head thrown back, her hair spilling in a glorious swirl of rich color. Her eyes were closed, and she had a tiny smile on her lips as Matt massaged her feet. She wiggled her toes rapturously. "Umm, that feels wonderful. Where did you get such terrific hands?"

"Practice," he taunted.

She quirked a brow. "Oh, really!"

Matt grinned at her and maneuvered the subject back on track. "What else did you do today?"

"Not much. I looked at wallpaper samples most of the afternoon. I'm doing the new offices for the Jamison Corporation. The chief executive officer's wife thinks her husband's firm will make millions more with impressive wallpaper and rosewood desks. I don't think it's occurred to her that he's able to afford all of these fancy new furnishings because he's done so well just by using his brain."

Matt waited for her to mention the trip to the doctor, but no matter how he probed she simply told him more tales about her difficult clients. When she started enthusiastically describing the paint chips she'd picked out for the Jamison Corporation rest rooms, he decided she was clearly avoiding any mention of the doctor visit. He wanted to shout at her in frustration.

His concern grew when she made the same trip at the same time again on Wednesday and Friday.

But when she left the doctor's office on Friday she didn't go on to see a client or to check out furniture stores as she had every other day until Matt felt like he'd seen enough to decorate a dozen homes. She went across town to the hospital where they'd been on Saturday. Matt's heart thudded against his ribs as he watched her walk into the building, her shoulders hunched against the bitter cold wind, her hair sparkling with red highlights in the midmorning sun.

Torn apart by the look of fear he could read on her face even from a distance, he moved closer, only barely restraining himself from calling out to her. She walked inside and he followed her as she went briskly through the maze of corridors. Her steps slowed at last, then finally faltered. She hesitantly approached the door at the end of the hallway, then stood peering through the window, an anguished expression on her face.

He could see her bite her lower lip. Tears slid down her cheeks as he saw her mouth, "No. Please, God. No."

Matt felt an incredible pain wrench his gut as Meg apparently challenged her demons and won. He watched her take a deep breath, square her shoulders, open the door and slip inside.

Matt waited for a few minutes to see if she'd return, then edged closer to read the sign on the door. As he did, all of his breath whooshed out of him and he closed his eyes against the pain. He opened them again and touched his fingers to the sign, like a blind man desperately seeking answers.

DIALYSIS UNIT. The words told him nothing...or far too much. Inside, he saw the patients lying back in reclining chairs, blankets tucked around them. They were hooked up to machines that slowly cleansed their blood of impurities. It looked to him like a high tech torture chamber. Yet he knew for these people it represented life in the form of a day-to-day struggle against the failure of their kidneys. But what did it mean to Meg?

She was talking to one of the nurses. Her shoulders were still straight, but her hands were clenched into fists at her side. The nurse took her to one of the machines, introduced her to the patient there—a young girl who was watching television. The girl's pale lips curved into one of the most appealing, heart-breaking smiles Matt had ever seen. Meg chatted with her for a few minutes, exchanged a few more words with the nurse, then started for the door. Matt moved back, but didn't leave.

When Meg came into the hall, she leaned against the wall and closed her eyes, her face drained of color. A tremor of icy fear swept through Matt, followed by compassion. It didn't matter that she hadn't told him everything. It only mattered that she was hurting, that she needed him.

He went to her and put his arms around her. Instinctively, she turned into his embrace, her face buried against his shoulder. He could feel her whole body trembling with sobs.

"Oh, Meg," he whispered, running his fingers through her hair, caressing her neck. With one hand he tried to massage away the tension in her shoulders. "It's okay. Whatever it is, it's okay."

Suddenly, she tried to inch away from him. She gazed up at him with startled eyes, as if realizing for the first time who was holding her and that their meeting was no accident.

"You've been spying on me!" she said slowly, her voice filled with disbelief. Then as the impact finally sank in, she shouted, "Damn you, Matt. How could you do it? How could you spy on me?"

She was pummeling him on the chest in an attempt to break his embrace. All of her pain and anger was directed at him, but he suspected much of it had to do with things he was only beginning to imagine. He held her tighter until all of the fight seemed to drain out of her and she collapsed against him.

"Yes," he admitted gently. "Call it spying, if you want to, but I had to know what you were hiding from me. Why have you been going to the doctor? Why are you here?"

"I have diabetes, Matt. I had a bad reaction the other day. You know that."

"You told me that hypoglycemic reactions are not uncommon, particularly if you're not careful."

"That's true."

"Then there has to be more to it," he said, waiting patiently. "You've been to see Dr. Mitchell three times this week and now you're here. I'll ask you again: why?"

"It's nothing for you to worry about," she said defiantly.

"I don't believe you."

"That's too bad."

His gaze was relentless, and Meg's defiance eventually faltered. Matt sensed the weakening of her resolve and said gently, "Tell me, Meg. Please."

"I'm dying," she finally whispered, crumpling into his arms. Tear-filled eyes gazed up at him in still-stunned disbelief. "I'm only twenty-seven years old, Matt, and I'm dying."

Eight

What?''

Matt's voice came out in a whisper and the expression of anguish and horrified incredulity in his eyes was something Meg had hoped never to see. She recognized the look. It reflected the way she'd reacted on the day a few weeks earlier when Dr. Mitchell had told her why she'd been feeling so poorly.

"For one thing, my dear, you're anemic," the doctor had said.

"Can't you give me an iron supplement?"

"I can, but I'm afraid that won't do it." His tired gaze had become compassionate. "Meg, I'm going to be honest with you. These symptoms you're having—the loss of appetite, the headaches and nausea—they're not good. The tests show a problem with your kidneys. Without treatment right now, you're going to get worse. Much worse.''

"I'm going to die?" she'd asked in a hushed tone.

"If we don't take corrective action, yes."

She'd heard the rest of Dr. Mitchell's words, but she hadn't understood at first. It was all so unreal that all she felt was an aching numbness. Then she'd been swept by a horrible sense of rage at the unfairness of it all.

By the time she'd met Matt, she'd felt little more than resignation at the cruel joke fate was playing on her, robbing her of life just when she had so much to live for. Even while they'd been together, she'd begun tying up the loose ends of her life—writing a will, negotiating for the sale of her business. She'd gone about it with methodical, unfeeling determination, vowing that no one else would have to take care of things after she had gone. It was a matter of pride to her that she be remembered for the strength with which she'd faced her greatest challenge. Duncan had taught her all about the Blake honor.

It had been a point of honor, too, to break it off with Matt before he had to suffer as well, but that had obviously been a naive, wishful idea. Still wrapped in her own sense of disbelief and pain, she hadn't had the courage to let him go. She should have known she could never keep anything this important from a man who loved her with Matt's intensity, especially a man who was used to digging for facts.

But Meg hadn't been able to tell Matt goodbye. Her halfhearted effort to separate from him hadn't accomplished a thing, except perhaps to infuriate Matt. She had tried avoiding him as much as he would allow, but she'd given him a key to her town house. It was impossible to shut him out without changing the locks, which she couldn't bring herself to do. As a result, he was always waiting when she came in from work, watching her with those catlike green eyes that were filled with questions. She'd tried to maintain a distance between them, but Matt had fought her every step of the way by using his wit and charm. When those failed, he'd simply reached out to touch her gently and she'd willingly surrendered into his waiting arms, her body on fire, her heart filled with love.

It was, she'd finally realized only this morning, hopeless to try to reject a man who didn't want to be rejected—especially a man you loved—not unless you possessed far more strength than she had. You needed to say the words, to tell him with absolute finality to go, and Meg couldn't force those irrevocable words passed her reluctant lips.

Now it was too late. The truth was out.

"Come with me," Matt said, his voice harsh, his eyes dark with pain. He half dragged her down the corridor, peering in doorways, finally stopping in the first lounge he came to. He punched a couple of quarters into the vending machine for coffee, gave her a cup and sipped at his own. His gaze explored her from head to toe as if he was looking for a sign that would contradict the awful words she had just blurted out.

But Meg knew she was beginning to look like hell, and there was no contradiction in her appearance. Her mirror's stark image, before she altered it with deft makeup artistry, was of a woman who was dying bit by bit, all of the vitality slowly draining out of her. Matt loved her too much not to see through the sham of eye shadow and blusher.

"Okay, Meg. I want to hear it," he said, sitting beside her, clinging tightly to her hand. "All of it."

Meg began haltingly, finally telling him everything that she knew. She explained that the diabetes was more severe than any of them had realized. It had damaged her kidneys until they were barely functioning.

"It's all those tiny blood vessels in there, I guess. Diabetes can play havoc with them, though most people go for years without ever suffering the extensive damage I have."

"How did it happen?" Matt asked, his voice breaking.

Meg looked at him wearily, her blue eyes shimmering with unshed tears. "Don't you think I've asked myself and Dr. Mitchell that a million times in the last couple of weeks? Why me? It's the question every person who's just been given a death sentence asks. I don't know the answer. No one does."

"When did you find out?"

"Right before I met you. That's why I didn't want to get involved." She reached up and caressed his cheek. "I tried to fight it, Matt. I really did."

Matt grinned at her ruefully. "So I recall. But that's all over now. No more pretending. No more secrets." His body shook, and he brushed furiously at a tear that was rolling down his cheek. When he'd regained control, he took her hands in his again and promised solemnly, "We'll get through this, babe."

"Matt, it's not your problem."

He cupped her chin in his hand and gazed into her eyes. Meg saw more love than any woman had a right to hope for in the depths of those eyes. "Don't ever let me hear you say that again," he said vehemently. "I love you, Meg Blake, and there's no way in hell I'm walking out on you now."

"You should."

"Remember me? I'm the guy who doesn't like to play by the rules."

"I don't deserve you," she said softly.

"You deserve everything life has to give, and I'm going to do my damnedest to see that you get it."

"Everything?" she queried, her mouth curving up at the corners in a smile that didn't quite make it to her eyes.

"Everything."

"Then I would like it very much if you would take me home and make love to me. I need to have your arms around me."

"I'd like that very much, too," Matt said quietly, pulling her to her feet and settling her coat snugly around her shoulders. Then they walked slowly out of the hospital, Matt's arm already tight around her.

At Meg's town house, he stripped away her clothes with an urgency fed by desperation. He needed to feel the warmth of her skin, the violence of her ecstatic shudders. He needed, more than anything, to know that she was alive.

They made love with a fierce abandon, then again with sweet gentleness. And when Meg's skin was flushed and covered with a sheen of perspiration, Matt cradled her in his arms and murmured again and again just how much he loved her.

"I won't let you go," he said, knowing that his determined words were futile if it had been willed otherwise.

"You may not have a choice," Meg said gently, her fingers resting in the dark, passion-dampened swirl of hairs on his chest.

"There must be something we can do, some treatment."

Meg hesitated, refusing to meet his gaze. At last she said, "No, Matt. There's nothing."

"I can't accept that. I'm going to the doctor with you," he said. "When's your next appointment?"

"Matt, you can't. What's the point?"

He sighed and ran a hand along the curve of her bare hip, the length of her slender thigh. His eyes met hers solemnly. "I guess the point is that I need to hear from him that it's hopeless."

Meg tried to talk him out of it, but he was adamant. Matt assumed she was trying to protect him. He didn't catch the nervousness or, if he noticed it at all, he attributed it to her very natural fear about her fate.

Hell, he was terrified. She must be completely twisted up inside and yet she maintained a cheerful facade for him.

It never occurred to him over the rest of the weekend that she was hiding something. She seemed so open, so relieved now that he knew the truth. She filled those two days with enchantment, a never-ending game of hide-and-seek in which the prize was always spectacular passion. This was Meg as the child she'd never been. This was Meg as the exciting woman she'd become. This was Meg as he'd grown to love her.

"Meg, where are you?"

Her mysteriously muffled voice drifted up to him, luring him downstairs.

"Meg?"

"You're getting warmer."

"Where the devil are you?"

A musical giggle was his answer.

"You're going to be sorry for this."

"I don't think so."

"Dammit, you're not in the living room or the den or the kitchen, but I know you're down here."

"That's very good, detective."

"The closet?" The door was ajar. He threw it all the way open. His eyes widened. "Why are you standing in the closet in a fur coat?"

"Come and see," she suggested in a throaty taunt.

Matt's heartbeat accelerated. "Meg, do you have anything on under that coat?"

His fingers caught the edge and drew the coat back. "Oh, my God! Isn't that lingerie illegal?"

"Only if you wear it in public with nothing over it."

"You don't have anything over it."

"I have on a fur coat," she corrected very solemnly, though her eyes were sparkling brightly with amusement and sensuality.

"Not anymore," he said as he slid the coat off her shoulders, scooped her into his arms and carried her into the living room. They made love in front of the fire. Meg continued to be playful, her touch light and taunting. She was the perfect foil for Matt's somber mood. As they were swept into a whirlwind of pleasure, they were so caught up in the present they had no time for worries about the future. Matt knew she had planned it to happen exactly that way.

In just the same way, on Sunday morning she followed him into the shower and used her soapy hands on his slick, responsive flesh to make him forget all about the good intentions he'd had about stopping by his office. Later there was a meal of paté and caviar in front of the fire. Still later there was a chess game in which Meg beat him by rubbing her foot along his calf until he was thoroughly distracted.

"Checkmate," she said gleefully.

"You don't play fair," he grumbled, but his words were lost as she slid into his lap and covered his mouth with her own. Her arms twined around his neck and Matt moaned with pleasure as his body came alive once more.

Late in the night, thoroughly exhausted, he brushed a kiss across her cheek and murmured, "I know what you're up to, lady."

"You do?"

He nodded sagely. "You think I'll be so worn out by morning, I won't be able to go with you to your doctor's appointment."

Her eyes flashed with indignation. "Matthew Flanagan, I never thought any such thing."

He grinned at her. "Good. Then you won't be disappointed that it's not going to work."

Meg sighed, curved her body tightly against his and fell asleep. As tired as he was, it took Matt far longer to quiet his troubling thoughts and drift off. When he did, his dreams were filled with images of Meg leaving him behind. He woke up trembling, his body icy cold. He reached for Meg, but she was already up and gone. For a moment he panicked and then her heard her downstairs.

Breakfast was a silent affair, neither of them wanting to discuss Meg's doctor appointment nor able to think of anything else to say. An hour later, they were in the doctor's office.

"I'm glad you finally told him, Meg," the doctor said as he shook Matt's hand.

"I didn't exactly tell him. He played private detective and found out on his own. The next time I fall in love, I think I'd better choose an accountant with no curiosity." The expression that played about her lips was wry.

"However it happened, I'm still glad. You need support now." He regarded Matt speculatively. "Maybe you can talk some sense into her."

Matt's brows lifted quizzically as he caught Meg's almost imperceptible shake of her head. The doctor ignored her and went on to describe Meg's condition in thorough detail. Clinically, there were few variations from what Meg had already told him.

"Of course, there are things we could do," he went on with what Matt interpreted as cautious optimism. "We have two options at this stage."

"Options? I thought this was terminal."

"If the condition is allowed to progress unchecked, yes, it is. But let's just say there are some delaying tactics we can take. Meg doesn't seem to want to try them."

"Why the hell not?" Matt exploded, regarding her incredulously. Meg was fidgeting uncomfortably in her chair, refusing to meet his gaze at first, then scowling at him defiantly.

"They're not feasible for me," she said flatly. She glared at Dr. Mitchell. "There's no point in discussing them."

"The doctor seems to think they offer some hope. I want to hear about them." Matt countered just as obstinately.

For a change, Dr. Mitchell listened to him, rather than Meg. "First," he said, "there's dialysis. Do you understand how that works?"

"I think so," Matt said.

"Well, it could take over for Meg's kidneys for a while, buy us some time."

"I won't be hooked up to a damn machine. I saw what that was like on Friday. You were there, Matt. You saw it, too. I'd rather be dead!"

"Meg, you can't mean that!" Matt protested.

"I do mean it. It's my life, what there is of it, and I won't live that way."

Meg was trembling and Matt tried to put aside his own building outrage and sense of frustration. He reached over and took her hand. "Calm down, love, and I will, too. Let Dr. Mitchell finish." He looked at the physician. "You said there was another option."

The older man nodded. "Best of all, of course, would be a transplant. Meg is young. She'd be a good candidate, especially if we could get a close relative as a donor. She'd be able to live a normal life for some time. She's refused that, too."

"You mean a transplant could save her life, and she won't have one?" He regarded Meg incredulously. "What the hell is wrong with you? He's giving you a chance to live."

"You missed the part about the transplant being best from a close relative."

"I didn't miss a damn thing," he flared. "I thought you loved me, Meg."

"I do," she said, scowling at him. She couldn't understand the depth or direction of his anger. She could understand his pain, even his rage against the reality of what was happening, but not this expression of betrayal she saw on his face. It was her life that was ending, not his. "I never asked you to be with me, Matt. You chose to stay. You knew the risks."

"Not this one," he protested. "I didn't know this one. I didn't know the woman I love was such a coward that she wouldn't at least try to live."

Meg felt as though he'd struck her. "How dare you say that? I'd do anything to live."

"Anything except what the doctor's suggesting."

"Grandfather's too old to be a donor and I won't go to my parents, Matt. I can't."

"Then I'll go. If you won't save yourself, then I guess it's up to me."

"If you go, I'll never forgive you," she threatened furiously.

Matt met her flashing eyes calmly. "If I don't, I'll never forgive myself."

Nine

Meg stormed out of Dr. Mitchell's office in a rage. Matt was so damn bullheaded! He was trying to take over her life. He was no better than her parents, determined to smother her, unwilling to let her make her own decisions. She had every right to choose the quality of her life for whatever time she had left. She even had the right to decide to die, she fumed as furious sobs wracked her body.

Oblivious to the curious stares of passersby, she paused to dig in her handbag for a tissue, then wiped her eyes. She thought about Matt, about how much joy he'd brought into her life and realized how badly she wanted to hold on to that. Didn't he understand that she wanted desperately to live, too? Especially now.

But, as she saw it, the alternatives were unacceptable. What kind of life would they have if she spent so many of her waking hours tied to a machine? She'd been awed by the bravery of the patients she'd seen at the hospital on Friday, but she didn't think she had it in her to be like them. She had only just discovered her independence. She couldn't relinquish it now, even if it gave her a few extra months.

As for the transplant, it was impossible. She had cut all ties to her parents, insisted that she could manage her own life. They would see now just how badly she had failed and throw her actions back in her face. She could hear her father accusing her of not taking her insulin, of not adhering to her diet, of not acting responsibly. They would feel certain that this was her fault, that if she'd only listened to them, it would not be happening.

No, she vowed, she could never ask her parents to submit to the testing and surgery Dr. Mitchell had suggested.

You don't have to, she reminded herself. Matt's gone to ask for you. Meg's lips pressed together in a furious frown. How could he? How could he so blatantly defy her wishes? The man was even more headstrong than her grandfather.

You're not being fair, she admitted to herself as she walked briskly. You can hardly fault Matt for wanting to help you live. She sighed deeply.

She wandered aimlessly for hours, her hands icy cold even in her lined gloves. The wind whipped her hair in her face. Eventually, she made her way all the way back to her town house, her body thoroughly chilled, her thoughts still whirling. A hot cup of tea, sipped at the kitchen table with Ginger at her feet, worked its usual magic, warming her and calming her down, allowing her to think more clearly.

Reluctantly she finally faced the fact that her outrage at Matt's imperious actions was really a smoke screen to hide her fear. What really terrified her was the possibility that Matt wouldn't succeed in his quest for help from her parents. After all that she had done to hurt them by leaving, why should they help her now? More than anything it was fear and foolish pride that had made her unwilling to approach them herself. She wondered if, after six years, they had forgiven her. Did they finally understand why she'd had to cut herself loose from the silky bonds of their love?

After the tea had taken the chill off, she started a roaring blaze in the fireplace and tried to settle down with a book. Unable to concentrate on the intricately spun mystery, she finally let it fall to her lap. She needed someone to talk to, someone who understood her and, after hesitating for several minutes, she called her grandfather for moral support. Maybe it was about time she started leaning on those she loved just a little. It was wrong, perhaps even selfish, to keep shutting them out. She shrugged wryly. Maybe it was time she *really* grew up.

"I've told Matt everything. He wasn't one bit pleased about my hiding it from him."

"But he's standing by you, isn't he?" Duncan sounded as though he might throttle Matt if he didn't. Meg's lips twitched slightly in amusement.

"You knew he would."

"I'd hoped so. I've always thought Matt was a fine man. Is he there now?"

"No. He's gone on a mission."

"A mission? What the devil does that mean? Is he off on some stupid case? Why isn't he there with you now when you need him?"

"No. He's not out on a case." She took a deep breath. "He's gone to see Mother and Father."

"Oh, I see." To Meg's amazement his voice held little surprise. In fact he sounded relieved, though he added, "I take it you don't approve."

"I'm still not sure exactly what I feel. At first I was livid, but maybe what he's doing is for the best. Maybe they have a right to know."

"Of course they have a right to know you're not well," Duncan growled. "But I'm sure Matt knows how things are between you and your parents, so I doubt he'd risk your wrath just to give them an update on your health. What's the rest of it, Margaret Ann?"

When her grandfather spoke to her in that no-nonsense tone, Meg knew there was no point in equivocating. He'd goad her until she blurted out the rest of it anyway. She might as well get it over with.

"He's going to tell them that I need a kidney transplant. If I have one, I could live."

Duncan sucked in his breath. "My God, child, why didn't you say something sooner?"

"I couldn't." Meg choked back a sob. "I was too afraid they wouldn't help."

"My dear girl, of course your parents will be there for you. We all will."

"I don't know, Grandfather. I hurt them badly."

"I can't believe you'd think such a thing. You're still their own flesh and blood. In the end, that's all that really counts."

"I hope they see it that way. I don't think I could bear it if they didn't at least come back with Matt."

"They'll come, child. They'll come. Would you like me to drive over and wait with you?"

Meg sighed. "No. I'll be okay. I just needed to hear your voice. I feel better now."

"I'm here for you anytime."

"I know, Grandfather. Thank you."

When she hung up, Meg felt as though her nerves had been stretched more tautly then any circus tightrope. She pulled the vacuum cleaner out of the closet. Ginger ran and hid under the sofa. The dog remained out of sight as Meg vacuumed the entire downstairs, which her once-a-week maid had done only that morning. When she'd finished that task, she scrubbed the already spotless kitchen floor, then went upstairs and began cleaning out her closet. Ginger came out of hiding and followed, finding a comfortable spot at the foot of Meg's bed.

Meg approached the task with cold-blooded determination, throwing out anything she no longer wore, folding it neatly to be given to charity. She fingered the delicate silk of her spring dresses and wondered if she would be around to wear them. The possibility that she might not hit her like a sharp blow to the stomach.

"Oh, my God," she murmured as the reality sank in. For all of her tough talk and cool demeanor, it was a reality she had never before faced deep in her gut. She had been intellectualizing it, not feeling it. Now she allowed herself to feel the pain, to let the tendrils of anguish reach from her head to her heart, curling tighter and tighter.

Suddenly she was overcome with rage. She yanked the dresses out of the closet and hurled them on the bed. Finding a pair of scissors, she shredded them one by one. Her body trembled as she ripped off sleeves and slashed them from top to bottom. Soon hot, salty tears were spilling down her cheeks unchecked and she sank down in the middle of the colorful pool of material, her fists beating on the floor until her knuckles were scraped and bruised. Ginger ran in excited circles around her, darting in to lick at her tear-stained face.

"Damn! Damn! Damn!"

Her shouted curses mingled with Ginger's frantic barking and seemed to mock her useless outburst as they echoed through the empty house. When her rage was spent at last, her sobs finally trailed off into a whimper, and she wrapped her arms around the worried dog, burying her face in Ginger's thick coat. She forced herself to stop crying with the same inner strength that made her get out of bed every morning, even when she wanted most to curl up and hide.

Tonight, though, as shadows filled the room, she gave in to temptation, crept into the bed, pulled a blanket around her and went to sleep. At least it would be a temporary escape from pain and self-pity.

Ginger, defying the rules, jumped onto the bed and inched closer and closer to Meg's back, tilting her head as if waiting for the order to "get down." When it didn't come, she put her head on her paws and went to sleep, too.

Across the Potomac River in Virginia, Matt pulled up in the circular driveway of a modest brick colonial-style home on a tree-filled corner lot. The tree branches were now mostly bare, though a few red and yellow leaves still clung to life. It must have been a lovely home to grow up in, he thought, especially in summer when the trees shaded the house and flowers bloomed in the gardens. He glanced around, wondering for a moment if the rose trellis to the left of the front door was the one from which Meg had fallen. An image of her enchanting face flashed into his mind and renewed his sense of purpose.

He'd called the Blakes from a pay phone right after leaving the doctor's office. Jackie Blake had been startled, but she had agreed to see him at six. Since making the call he'd been driving around trying to gather his thoughts and restore his composure. He was afraid he'd come on like old man Blake leading his troops into war. From everything he'd learned recently about Meg's parents, if he did that, they'd toss him right back out on his ear without listening to a word. Meg's future was too important for him to risk making that mistake.

By the time he rang the doorbell, he still couldn't imagine what to expect from the Blakes, but he was prepared to give a quietly impassioned plea on Meg's behalf. No matter how embittered they were, surely they wouldn't turn their backs on their only child.

The woman who opened the door to him was slender and stylish in a gold silk hostess outfit, her hair a softly styled arrangement of auburn curls that framed a still-pretty face. Her eyes were as blue as Meg's, though they were clouded now by concern. The physical resemblance between the two women was striking. Matt wondered if they shared the same strength of character.

"Mrs. Blake, I'm Matt Flanagan."

She shook his hand warmly and gave him a tentative, hopeful smile. "How do you do? You said on the phone you were a friend of Meg's."

"That's right."

"We..." Her voice broke. "We don't hear from her. Is she okay?"

He touched her hand and spoke gently. "No, Mrs. Blake. I'm afraid not. That's what I wanted to talk to you about. Is your husband here?"

"Perhaps it would be better if you told me. Jonathan is still very angry with Meg. He was furious that I told you to come."

"I understand that, but I think it would be better if I spoke with both of you."

Apparently she sensed his determination because she relented. "Of course. Come with me. Jonathan is in the living room." She led the way, then introduced him to a man who was as tall and broad-shouldered as Duncan and whose chin was set just as stubbornly.

"I don't know why you're here, Mr. Flanagan. Meg doesn't want anything to do with us. She made that very plain. If she's gone and fouled up her life, it's nothing to do with us."

"Meg has not *fouled up her life*, at least not the way you mean. She's a very successful interior designer. She has a lovely home. But she is in trouble and she does need you."

Jonathan Blake regarded him skeptically. "Then why isn't she here herself?"

"Because she's afraid, maybe even ashamed of how she's treated you. I don't know exactly. I do know that she's desperately in need of your love and support." He decided not to mince words. "Meg is dying."

Jackie Blake's eyes widened, then filled with tears. "My baby! Dear God, no!"

"I don't believe you," Jonathan barked. "What kind of sick person are you to come here with an outrageous lie like that? Get out of my house. Meg's already caused us enough pain. Can't you see what you're doing to her mother with your lies? I want you to go."

Matt waited patiently through his tirade. "Not until you've heard me out. If you don't believe me, you can call your father. He'll confirm all of this."

Jackie Blake's eyes flashed as she faced her husband defiantly. "I'm all right, Jonathan. I want to hear what he has to say."

"Mr. Blake?" Matt said softly.

Jonathan seemed to struggle with himself. "Okay," he said at last. "Get on with it."

Matt explained everything about Meg's condition that he knew. By the time he'd finished, tears were streaming down her mother's face. For all of his initial hardened attitude, Jonathan Blake appeared stunned now, almost physically diminished. Every bit of his bluster was gone. He looked exactly the way Duncan had on the day he'd sent Matt to find Meg.

"You're sure about this?" Jonathan said at last, obviously still willing it to be a terrible lie. Matt knew exactly how he felt. He'd stared at the ceiling in Meg's bedroom through the last two endless nights praying that when morning came he'd find it had all been only a nightmare.

"I wouldn't be here, if I weren't. I just came from her doctor's office. Meg needs that transplant. Are you going to be there for her?"

"She'll have to come to us," Jonathan said, clinging stubbornly to the hardened attitude that had apparently gotten him through the last six years. "She's the one who walked out of here, rejected her own parents."

"And you want her to pay for it?" Matt said. "You want her to beg for forgiveness? Is that so important that you'd rather see her die?"

It was Jackie Blake who answered him. "No, of course not. What do you want us to do?"

"Go to her. I understand what your husband is saying. I know you may feel that Meg should be making the first move, since she's the one who walked out, but you have to understand that she can't bring herself to do it."

"Once we're there, do you honestly think it will be possible to put all of the anger and bitter words behind us?" Jonathan said skeptically. "You weren't around when she left. We all said some pretty terrible things. Meg told us we'd ruined her life and we told her she was an ungrateful, spoiled brat. That was just the tip of the iceberg. She broke her mother's heart."

He faced Matt squarely, his eyes shadowed with pain. "And mine."

"I honestly don't know if you can wipe away the words or the years of separation," Matt replied. "But you can at least try to work through your differences, maybe understand what happened. Even if you can't, even if the anger and pain go too deep, tell her that you'll do this for her."

He stared at Jackie Blake and then at her husband before saying softly, "She's your daughter. Please don't let her die."

"We'll come, Mr. Flanagan. But we'll need some time to pull ourselves together," Jackie Blake said decisively, drawing on some inner reserve of courage. Matt thought she seemed almost startled to have discovered it. She had dried her tears and had gone to her husband and was holding his hand in a white-knuckled grasp.

"I don't want Meg to see us like this," she said stoutly, regarding her husband pointedly. "She needs our strength now. Not our tears or recriminations."

"Come over tomorrow. That will be soon enough. I think Meg will need some time, too."

"We'll be there at noon," she promised.

"Mr. Blake?"

"Jonathan, please," Mrs. Blake pleaded.

He nodded at last, and Matt started toward the door. Then he paused and went back. "There's one more thing you should know. Meg wasn't happy about my coming to see you. I don't know how she'll react to your being there."

"It doesn't matter, Mr. Flanagan. I don't know what impression Meg has given you about us, but we've always loved her. Maybe too much. I think that's what drove her away," Mrs. Blake said. She gazed at Matt wistfully. "Do you think it's too late to make her see that we only did what we thought was best?"

He squeezed her hand reassuringly. "No. I think she's finally ready to listen to you. She was a rebellious girl back then. Now she's a mature, sensitive woman, who is very, very frightened."

Matt felt the first stirrings of hope as he drove back to Meg's house. When he arrived, he found her still asleep, Ginger beside her, the destroyed clothing scattered on the floor by the bed. The sight of those dresses made him want to weep, but he quietly picked them up and took them downstairs to the trash. Then he returned and nudged Ginger off the bed and carefully lowered himself beside Meg. When he wrapped her in his embrace, she moaned softly and snuggled closer. Matt studied her beloved face, forcing himself not to touch the dark smudges under her eyes.

"Oh, babe, I do love you so," he whispered, burying his face in her neck. Eventually, he drifted to sleep.

When Meg awoke, the first thing she felt was a wave of pleasure at finding herself wrapped in Matt's arms. Then she remembered where he had been and her breath caught in her throat. If he was here beside her, obviously her parents had not come. They had rejected his plea. They had taken her at her word six years ago and never planned to see her again. They didn't care if she died. To them she was already dead.

Once more her fear took the form of anger and she jabbed Matt awake with a sharp poke in the stomach. He blinked awake instantly and stared at her in astonishment.

"What..." His voice was befuddled. "Why'd you do that?"

"Damn you," she said fiercely. "Damn you, Matt Flanagan."

He smiled at her wanly. He'd hoped she would calm down when she'd had time to think things through. Obviously she hadn't, and perhaps that was better.

"I'm glad to see your temper's in good form," he said with forced cheer. "Because we're in for one hell of a fight, Meg Blake."

Now it was her turn to blink. "We are?"

"We sure are. We're going to save your life."

Instantly, her eyes filled with hope. "My parents?" she asked tremulously.

"They will be here tomorrow."

"Even my father?"

"Yes."

She closed her eyes just as a tear slid down her cheek. Matt kissed it away.

"No more tears, babe. From now on we have more important things to do."

Ten

In the morning before Meg was awake, Matt crept downstairs and called Duncan to tell him what was happening.

"I think you should be here, sir."

"No, son. This is between Meg and her parents. They don't need an audience, especially me. It would only infuriate Jonathan to find me there."

"He's already furious. He doesn't really want to come. What if he starts ranting and raving? I don't know if Meg can take it."

Duncan chuckled. "Give her some credit. Meg's a Blake through and through. She'll be able to handle Jonathan. In fact, I'd give almost anything to see it."

"Then come."

"No," he repeated adamantly. "And I think you should leave, too. I know you love her, but this is something Meg needs to do on her own. Her life's getting away from her, son. Let her feel as though she's in control of something. Let her know you believe in her."

Matt could see the wisdom in what Duncan was saying, but the prospect of leaving Meg alone when he didn't know what to expect from the Blakes worried him.

"I'll see how she seems this morning," he said at last. "If she's strong enough, I'll do as you say."

"Don't rush to the rescue, Matt," Duncan warned. "Make sure you give her the chance to be strong."

That was easier said than done. When Meg awoke, her nervousness and almost childlike hope nearly tore Matt in two. To see this normally self-confident, courageous woman so vulnerable was a heart-wrenching experience. It convinced him more than ever that the possibility of a family reconciliation was almost as important as the outcome of the transplant discussion.

"Stay here a little longer," Matt suggested, when Meg started to get up. "They won't be here for hours."

"I have a lot to do. They've never been here before. I want to make sure everything's perfect."

"The house is spotless," he reminded her. "You saw to that yesterday. There isn't an ashtray out of place. The flowers are fresh. Are you planning on putting up new drapes?"

"Don't be sarcastic," she chided and circled his neck with her arms. "Oh, Matt, don't you see how important this is? It's the first time I've seen my parents in more than six years."

"Yes, I see," he said, though the pressure of her breasts against his chest made him want to roll her onto her back and make love to her yet again. Instead, he said, "What can I do to help?"

"Just come downstairs and keep me company, so I don't go nuts." She gave him an encouraging grin. "And I'll even let you make the coffee."

"Thank God. I'd hate to have you poison them after all this."

For the next few hours, Meg bustled around the kitchen, preparing hors d'oeuvres, throwing out every single one that didn't look cookbook-perfect, or giving it to Matt. He began to feel like a garbage disposal. Suddenly Meg's brow creased with a frown and she gave Matt a troubled look.

"Oh, dear, maybe this isn't enough. Do you think I should be fixing lunch, instead?"

"I don't think it matters what you fix."

"Of course it matters," Meg countered irritably. "I'm probably making all the wrong things. They'll think there are too many carbohydrates or too much salt or something."

She sank down on a chair across from him and gazed at him wearily. "Matt, maybe we should call this off. I'm not ready to see them yet."

He brushed a dusting of flour off the tip of her nose.

"Calm down. We're not calling anything off. These are your parents, not the king and queen of England. They're not going to care whether your china is chipped, your cheese straws are burned or your mushroom caps are properly stuffed and browned. They certainly aren't going to check out the nutritional breakdown of what you serve. They're coming because they care about you."

Meg regarded him hopefully. "I want to believe that, but how could they, after all I did to alienate them?"

"Trust me, love. They do. I think once you talk to them all of you will begin to understand what happened six years ago, and then you'll be able to put it behind you and go on. I was pleasantly surprised to discover that your parents aren't ogres." At least your mother isn't, he amended silently.

"I never said they were. What happened was my fault. They made me feel so helpless, and the only way I could cope with that was to leave."

"Well, you're not helpless now. They're going to respect you for what you've made out of your life."

Meg sighed and looked at Matt sorrowfully. "You're wrong."

His brow lifted quizzically. "How?"

"You're forgetting that I'm more helpless now than I ever was before."

"No, babe. You may be sick, but you are the strongest woman I know."

He stood up and drew her into his arms, his hands stroking her back, then cupping her bottom until she was perfectly fitted against him. She wriggled with pleasure and regarded him with amusement. "Are you, by any chance, trying to distract me, Matthew Flanagan?"

"Is it working?"

"It's working." Tingles of excitement were dancing along her nerves. Her face was flushed with color for the first time in several days and, though she knew it had to do with Matt's touch and the heat in the kitchen, she felt almost healthy. At times like these, when Matt's deliberately provocative sensuality drew her in, she was almost able to forget just how ill she was.

"Too bad we don't have time to go upstairs before they get here," Matt grumbled.

"I've never made love in the kitchen before," Meg suggested boldly. She thrilled to the familiar smoky desire she saw in his eyes and the frustration that was evident on his face. "Aren't you even the tiniest bit tempted?"

"Oh, I'm tempted all right," he said, pressing against her so she could feel the evidence for herself. "Unfortunately, I don't think we have time to explore this sudden desire you seem to have developed for kinky experimentation."

"If the doorbell rings, we could just ignore it."

He smacked her playfully on the bottom. "Are you trying to use me to duck out on this meeting?"

Meg's grin was rueful. "You know me too darn well."

Matt shook his head. "Not nearly as well as I'm going to," he said solemnly. "I'm going to spend a lifetime getting to know you."

"Is that a promise?"

"Count on it."

He was leaning toward her for a kiss that Meg very much needed when the doorbell actually did ring.

"Hold that thought," Matt said, but Meg was already looking toward the living room with frightened eyes.

"Will you get it?" she asked, her voice barely above a whisper.

Matt took her hand. "We'll get it together."

With Matt at her side, Meg felt strong enough to face anything. She gave him her brightest smile. It only wavered a little.

"Okay," she said valiantly, "let's go into battle."

Despite her show of bravado, Meg's heart was in her throat as she opened the door and stood facing her parents. Her mother was at the door, her expression anxious. Her father was still on the walk as if even now he was torn between going and staying.

Meg studied them closely as they came in and handed her their coats, her father carefully avoiding her eyes. She tried like crazy not to let that hurt. They had aged since she'd last seen them. Her father's thinning hair was grayer now, and he'd developed a slight paunch. He must hate that, she thought, before allowing her hungry gaze to fall on her mother. Other than the dark circles under her eyes and a few tiny wrinkles at the corners, she looked almost the same, her beauty skillfully preserved.

"Meg, darling," she said softly, lifting her arms tentatively.

The coats fell to the floor forgotten as Meg released a choked sigh and went swiftly into her mother's embrace. The two women clung to each other, Jackie Blake murmuring words of comfort. Meg realized then just how badly she'd needed her mother. No woman would ever grow too old for her mother's reassurances when she was sick.

It was Matt who finally picked up the coats, hung them in the closet and suggested that they go into the living room. Despite the warm scene between mother and daughter in the hallway, he knew things were far from settled. For one thing there was Jonathan's continued resistance, his cool silence and hardened expression. On the surface he had seemed unmoved by the sight of Meg, though Matt noticed a slight tremor in his hands, as though he had longed to reach out and touch his daughter himself.

Once they were all settled with coffee and the assortment of snacks Meg had prepared, Matt said, "I'm going out for awhile. I think you all should have some time alone."

"Matt, no," Meg said with such urgency that Matt almost relented. Then he recalled what Duncan had said.

"You can handle this," he reassured her. "I know you can."

Meg watched him leave with a sense of panic. She had no idea what she was supposed to say to bridge the gap created by six years of silence. She'd counted on Matt to guide the way, to serve as a buffer to the raw feelings that were being exposed after all this time. She gazed at her parents and realized they were just as nervous as she was. None of them seemed able to bring themselves to get down to the real reason for the meeting.

Like fighters stepping into the ring, they circled warily for some time, the conversation between Meg and her mother filled with inane chitchat about the weather—wasn't it awfully cold in November? About the crabmeat-stuffed mushroom caps—where had she found the recipe? And about the Redskins—would they make it to the Super Bowl? Meg's nerves were stretched to the very limit and she felt as though she might scream.

Instead, taking a deep breath and thinking of Matt, she brought the conversation to a head.

Staring directly at her father, who still hadn't spoken, she said, "I can see that you don't want to be here, Father, and I don't blame you. Maybe we should just forget this. After what I did, you don't owe me anything."

"Don't say that, Meg. Yes, we do," her mother said. "We didn't mean to, but we took so many years away from you trying to do what we thought was best for you. We never stopped to think about what you wanted. Let us try to give some of those years back."

"Wait just a minute," Jonathan said, his shoulders rigid with tension. "We didn't take anything away from her. We gave her a home, the best schools, the best medical care, expensive clothes, everything money could buy. She took every bit of that from us and then she told us to get lost. I think after all this time she owes us an apology, an explanation, something."

"This is no time for that," Jackie countered furiously. "Can't you put that silly pride of yours aside for one minute? It cost you your father. Don't let it cost you your child, too."

Jonathan's expression was startled. If Meg hadn't been so scared, she might have laughed. Her father was probably as surprised by his wife's arguing at all as he was by her words. Her mother had never disagreed with a thing her father had said in all the years she'd lived in their house.

"I don't know what you mean," Jonathan said, still seeming bemused. "I thought you agreed with me that Father was interfering."

"Yes, I'm sorry to say, I did. Now I realize that he was merely expressing an opinion about his granddaughter's well-being. We didn't have to act on it, though I wish to heaven we had. Then maybe none of this would have happened."

"So you're on his side now?"

"Oh, for goodness' sakes, Jonathan, why do there have to be sides? Your father made mistakes, too."

She scowled. "In fact, I wish he were here now, too. I have a few things I'd like to say to him. He should have known better. He should have put Meg ahead of that damn stiff-necked pride of his and told us both to take a flying leap. Instead, he retreated to his house in the country to sulk with nothing but his pride for company. I'm sick to death of the distorted Blake sense of pride and honor. What kind of honor is it that keeps families apart?''

Her fury finally wound down and she added softly, ''Can't we finally just concentrate on what's important: seeing that Meg gets well?''

''Well said, Jackie.''

Three pairs of startled eyes looked toward the doorway where Duncan was standing, his hair wind-blown, his cheeks flushed from the cold.

''You're absolutely right. I have behaved like a stubborn old goat, and so has my son. I think it's time enough to put that in the past.'' He gazed at Jonathan, and Meg saw a hint of vulnerability in his eyes as he asked, ''Isn't it, son?''

Jonathan seemed ready to argue, but he finally raised his hands in a gesture of surrender. ''I suppose.''

Shaken, Meg went to her father and knelt by his chair. She knew what this had cost him. She wanted to give him something in return, the apology he felt he deserved.

''I'm sorry, Father. I do owe you an explanation. I know I made you think I hated you, but that wasn't it at all. I only left because I needed to grow up. I was afraid if I stayed, I'd never know what life was really like.''

"But the things you said—the things you accused us of doing—"

"I was wrong. I should have tried to explain then, told you how out of control I was feeling. I didn't really blame you for wanting to protect me, but I had to say all of those awful things to make you angry enough to let me go. I was afraid if we just talked about it, you'd convince me to stay, to let you go on pampering me. I was so scared of being on my own, it wouldn't have taken much to make me stay. I knew I had to risk losing you to have a life of my own, to experience things for myself. Can't you understand that now?"

"Sure. I understand that you wanted your independence, but look where it got you," he muttered, despair making his voice ragged. "Just look where it got you."

Meg tried to swallow the lump in her throat. "Even if I'd stayed, I don't think you could have protected me from this. The only thing you can do is help me now."

She gazed at him beseechingly. "Will you?"

Jonathan's shoulders suddenly shook with sobs and after what seemed like forever, he gathered Meg in his arms. It made her feel as though she'd come home at last, and she had Matt to thank for it.

"Just tell me what we have to do, baby," Jonathan murmured. "Just tell me what we have to do."

For the first time in weeks Meg forgot the past and began to believe in the future.

Eleven

Jonathan's words got them over the first hurdle, but Meg realized that the reconciliation was by no means complete. Although he was willing to go through the endless testing for her, she still caught the wariness in his voice, the signs of bitterness he couldn't quite hide. He'd claimed to accept her explanation for her actions six years earlier, yet Meg knew that true forgiveness and understanding were a long way off. Only her mother had truly put the past behind her.

The next couple of weeks were filled with doctors' appointments and laboratory tests to determine if either of her parents were suitable transplant donors. Just as important, the hours they spent together gave them time to talk, to fill in the missing details of their lives, to get to know each other again.

One afternoon, Meg proudly showed them her offices. Her mother was entranced with the albums of pictures of the offices and homes she'd decorated.

"Darling, I'm so proud of you," she said, and suddenly it all seemed worthwhile to Meg. She realized how empty her success had seemed without her parents' approval.

"Jonathan, look at this," Jackie said. "Something like this would be just perfect for your law office. Why don't you have Meg come over and take a look?"

"If she wants to."

"I'd love to. Why don't we go this afternoon?"

"There's no rush."

Meg's excitement evaporated at his lack of enthusiasm. "Did you already have a decorator?"

"No, of course he didn't," her mother said, glaring at her husband. "This afternoon will be perfect, won't it, Jonathan?"

He shrugged. "Sure. Why not?"

Meg took along fabric samples and paint chips. She and her mother had a wonderful time considering and rejecting dozens of them before they finally settled on a combination that they liked.

"It's perfect," her mother exclaimed. "Understated elegance, don't you think so, Jonathan?"

"I think your husband has the same eye for that kind of stuff that I have," a voice interceded.

Meg's eyes brightened. "Matt! What are you doing here?"

"Marjorie told me where I'd find you. I thought maybe we could all go out to dinner."

"I thought we'd eat in tonight. I have everything planned."

He studied her closely. "Are you sure you feel up to cooking?"

"Absolutely, and mother said she'd help. Grandfather's coming, too. It's sort of an early Thanksgiving dinner since I may be in the hospital on the holiday."

"In that case, by all means, let's eat in. Do I get to carve the turkey? I'm very good with a knife."

"Maybe in the jungle, but I think we'll let Father do that. I want the turkey sliced, not gashed to bits. Besides, it's sort of a family tradition."

They had just said the blessing that night, when the call came from Dr. Mitchell.

"Meg, dear, I've just had word."

"And?" she said, her voice shaking. She held onto the phone so tightly her knuckles turned white.

"The tissue typing and other tests indicate that your father will be a good donor. The surgeons would like the two of you in the hospital on Sunday. As soon as I reach your father to confirm it, we'll make the arrangements."

"He's here now. I'll get him."

Meg was filled with a combination of anticipation and dread as she handed the phone to her father. He spoke quietly to the doctor for several minutes and then hung up. He stood staring straight ahead, then finally he held out his hand to Meg. "Well, kiddo, it looks like we're in this together."

She wrapped her arms around him. "I love you, Daddy."

Jonathan sighed deeply. "I love you, too." The words were spoken so softly she could hardly hear them, but he'd said them at last, and that was all that mattered.

On Saturday, Meg's last night before going into the hospital, Matt picked her up at her office where she'd insisted on going to finish up some details on the proposal for her father's office. She wanted the job done in time for his release from the hospital.

"Where are we going?" she asked as they drove into an unfamiliar part of the city.

"It's a surprise."

"What kind of surprise?"

He turned and lifted one brow.

"Oh, never mind," she grumbled.

Matt parked in front of a row of exclusive shops, and Meg's heart skipped a beat. There was a jewelry store in this block, as well as three outrageously expensive boutiques. Had Matt done something wildly extravagant? She hoped not. It would be awhile before she was ready to dazzle Washington in a new gown.

If ever. The frightening thought was there and gone before she could stop it. Refusing to admit to any more fears, she bit her lip and walked beside Matt as he marched purposefully down the street, passing most of the shops.

"In here," he said at last.

"But it's a house. Are we going to visit someone?"

"Not exactly."

"What exactly?"

"Meg, it's a surprise. You don't ask what a surprise is. You wait until it, well, until it surprises you."

"As long as it doesn't shock me," she muttered back at him. Matt rolled his eyes in exasperation and led her up the steps.

A minute later, the door was opened by a tiny, white-haired lady with sparkling brown eyes. When she recognized Matt, literally hundreds of wrinkles lifted in a smile that warmed Meg right down to her toes.

"Matthew, here you are at last. And this must be that young lady who's been keeping you away from me." Her eyes twinkled at Meg. "Pretty little thing. Much too pretty for Matthew. I ought to introduce you to my other nephew, Matthew's cousin. He's much better looking."

"You do and we're through, Nell Flanagan," Matt warned. He waved a bag of peppermints at her. "No more of these."

"Oh, posh-tosh, boy, I can buy my own mints."

Matt grinned at her and stuffed the bag back into his pocket. "Then I guess I'll just be keeping these."

"Hand 'em over and bring your young lady inside before she decides we're both loony as can be. You don't want her to run out on you, do you?"

Matt's gaze caressed Meg. "Oh, I'm not letting her get away," he said fervently. "Meg, in case you haven't guessed, this impossible lady is my aunt. Until you came along, she was the only woman besides Sally who could keep me in line."

Nell Flanagan's eyes sparkled with amusement as she clasped Meg's hand. "You keep this one on a tight leash, girl. Men have to be taught their place, if you're ever to have a moment's peace. Took me years to get my late husband trained."

Meg grinned at Matt. "Please," she said. "Tell me exactly what you did."

Matt glowered at the two of them. "Don't you dare," he growled, then suggested, "Show Meg the present I picked out for her."

"Oh, my dear, wait until you see," Nell said excitedly. "It's the best I have."

Meg's eyes were lit with curiosity as she followed Matt's aunt down a long corridor, then into the kitchen.

"Right out here," she said, leading them onto an enclosed porch which was dominated by a huge wooden box.

Meg walked over and peered in, her lips parting in a gasp of absolute delight. She dropped to her knees. "Oh, Matt, they're darling."

A sleek Irish setter was sprawled in the middle of the box with half a dozen golden-red puppies squirming around her. Meg held her hand down and several cold wet noses were pressed against it. One of the puppies latched onto a finger and tried sucking frantically.

Matt and Nell exchanged glances. "What did I tell you?" he said. "That's the one I picked out. I knew he had good taste."

He regarded Meg hopefully. "Do you think Ginger will mind having a roommate?"

"I think she'll be delighted." Meg got to her feet and hugged him. "What made you think of it?"

"I figured you couldn't possibly name this one Ginger, if Ginger were still alive. I think it's about time you found a new name for a pet."

"Interesting concept, but I think there's something more to this. What is it?"

Matt and his aunt exchanged glances and he said softly, "I thought it might give you an extra incentive to get well fast, if you knew you had a new puppy counting on you."

"Oh, darling. I already have all the incentive I need," she said, standing on tiptoe to kiss him. It was meant to be a gentle thank-you kiss, but it quickly escalated to much more. Tenderness turned to desire. Cautious exploration flared into passion. The warmth of the porch became hot, stifling, and Meg felt as though she'd been robbed of breath. It was, ironically, an exhilarating feeling. It was only after she'd luxuriated in it for several minutes that she remembered where she was. Suddenly embarrassed, she tried to free herself from Matt's embrace.

"Matt!"

"Umm!" His lips were burning against the cool flesh of her neck. Meg moaned, then protested again.

"Matt, stop. Please."

"Why?"

"Because we are not alone," she said dryly.

"I'll bet we are," he retorted.

Meg glanced around and discovered he was right. His aunt had vanished.

"Oh, this is awful. What will she think of me?" She started to go in search of her.

"She'll think that *we* are very much in love and she'll be right. Now come back here. It may be a while before we get to do this again."

Meg clasped her hands behind his neck and stared into his eyes. "Then let's go home and do it properly," she suggested softly.

"What a good idea!"

"Do you think your aunt will mind?"

"I think she'd be disappointed if we didn't. She's a big fan of romance."

Nell's expression was filled with amusement as Meg mumbled a hurried apology and tried to come up with a discreet excuse for their rapid departure.

"You just come back here soon to get that puppy of yours," she said, giving Meg a hug. She gave Matt a pointed look. "Next time maybe you'll be able to stay a little longer."

As soon as they were back on the street, Meg groaned and said, "She knew. She knew exactly why we were leaving."

"I told you she would."

"But, Matt, that's awful. She comes from another generation. They're not nearly as liberated. She must think I'm nothing but a tramp."

Matt's laugh rumbled from deep in his chest. "My dear woman, you've got to be kidding. When I told her I was bringing you over here tonight—your last night before going into the hospital—she told me I was a bigger fool than she'd imagined. If we hadn't left there when we did, she probably would have disowned me. It would have destroyed my reputation as a rake. She's always rather relished the thought that I was quite a ladies' man. She says she can hardly wait for the woman who tames me."

"Are you serious?"

"I am very serious."

She gazed up at him provocatively. "In that case, we'd better get home quickly and preserve your reputation."

The two of them were awake most of the night, sometimes making love, but mostly just holding each other. Neither could bring themselves to talk about what the days to come would bring. When they spent twenty minutes arguing about names for the puppy, Matt almost wished he hadn't gotten it. He wanted so badly to talk about the future, but every time he broached the subject, Meg put a restraining finger against his lips.

"Later, my love. The only thing we can count on is the present."

"But..."

She finally silenced him with a hungry, desperate kiss.

Matt thought about that kiss, as Meg was wheeled down the hospital corridor just over twenty-four hours later. That kiss, more than any of the words she had spoken, told him of her anxiety. She was terrified that there would be no tomorrows for her. For them. But she had refused to cast shadows on their last hours by talking about what might happen. As Matt and Duncan walked alongside the gurney, Matt wondered once more if he should have made her confront her fears. Surely there were words he could have said to comfort her, words to give her strength.

"You're a winner, child. Remember that," Duncan said, squeezing her hand and turning away before Meg could see the tears in his eyes. He went over to his son's stretcher and clasped Jonathan's hand. "God bless you, son."

Matt heard fragments of their whispered conversation.

"I never meant to hurt her or you, Father."

"I know that."

"Forgive me."

"The Lord's the one who deals in forgiveness. I just want you to know I love you."

"I love you, too."

Matt looked down and realized that Meg could hear them, too. She was crying. "Scared?"

"No. Happy," she said groggily. "It was awful feeling responsible for their separation."

"After today, you're going to have all the time in the world together." He kissed her, a lingering kiss that was meant to be a promise. "So will we."

"I hope so," she murmured as they pushed her toward the operating room. Just before the doors swung closed, she called out his name. Worried, Matt ran to her side. When he leaned close, she gave him a wobbly grin.

"I've decided on a name for the puppy."

He almost groaned. "What?"

"I'm going to call him Ginger Junior."

Matt did groan at that, but he thought he heard her laugh as the door closed. He held onto that sweet, joyful sound during the long wait.

Twelve

————

Matt then endured the longest hours of his life. It was far worse than sitting tensely in a jungle waiting for signs of enemy movements. He and Duncan paced restlessly, drank coffee and scowled at the clock. Only Jackie Blake seemed serene. In fact, she seemed to draw on some previously hidden strength to keep Matt and her father-in-law from falling apart. Matt was astonished at her bravery and grateful for her cheerful, optimistic presence.

The surgery lasted only a few hours, but it seemed like an eternity before the surgeon and Dr. Mitchell finally emerged from the operating suite.

"They're both doing just fine," Dr. Mitchell said. "We'll have to watch closely for complications and, in

Meg's case, for signs of rejection, but I'm expecting the rest to go smoothly.''

"When will we know about rejection?" Matt asked.

"Problems usually show up either immediately or sometime during the first three months. If she gets through that, then she'll have to stay on medication, but she should be able to lead a normal life.''

"When can we see them?" Jackie asked.

"I'd prefer it if you'd wait until tomorrow to see Jonathan. With Meg we'll have to wait a bit longer. I want her in isolation because of the immune system depressants we have her on. I don't want to risk any infections. Go home and get some rest.''

Matt's mouth turned down in a defiant slash. "I'm not leaving until I see her.''

Duncan put an arm around him. "The doc's in charge here, son. Not us." He glanced at the surgeon and promised, "We'll go home.''

Duncan insisted Matt come out to his place. "We'll drink some bourbon and tell war stories. It'll keep us both out of mischief.''

Matt's glance was filled with amusement. "You don't trust me to stay away, do you?''

"Your lack of patience has been demonstrated in the past,'' Duncan reminded him.

"And you're any better? You're champing at the bit to get into that room.''

"I'm not denying it. Maybe this way, though, we can both keep reminding each other that we're doing what's best for Meg.''

"How can it be best for her not to have her family around?" Matt growled.

"You heard the doctor. We could make her sick if we're carrying around any germs. Now come on, son. Do you want me to pull rank on you?"

Matt followed reluctantly. However, Duncan's expensive bourbon, his cook's superb lamb chops and their reminiscences didn't do a thing to banish the image of Meg all alone in her hospital room. As soon as he was sure Duncan had had time to get to sleep, Matt slipped out of the house and drove back to the hospital.

Feeling like a fugitive, he crept cautiously upstairs and started toward her room, promising himself he'd only peek in to be sure she was okay. When he saw someone walking toward him, he ducked into a linen closet and hid behind a cart filled with sheets, his heart pounding like a jackhammer. As soon as he heard the footsteps pass, he edged back into the corridor. He was only three rooms away, when a sturdy nurse with the demeanor of a Sherman tank stopped him.

"Visiting hours are long over, young man. Just where do you think you're going?" she demanded, blocking his path.

Matt flushed guiltily. "To see my fiancée," he said in a confident, persuasive tone that had been useful in getting him past many a reluctant secretary. He flashed his most beguiling smile.

She glowered at him. "That wouldn't be Miss Blake, would it?"

He nodded, suddenly feeling exactly like a small boy who'd just been caught with an illegal wad of bubble gum in his mouth. His smile faded. "She's okay, isn't she?"

"She's resting comfortably, which is more than I can say for the rest of us. I feel like I'm playing armed guard at Fort Knox tonight."

Matt quirked a brow quizzically.

"You're not the first visitor who's tried to sneak in," she explained.

"Oh?"

"If you won't go home where you belong, you might as well get yourself a cup of coffee in the cafeteria and join the other one in the waiting room." She waved a finger in his face. "And if either one of you try to sneak in there again tonight, I'll see that the doctor bans you permanently. Is that clear?"

Matt knew when he'd been defeated. He got the coffee and went back to the waiting room, where he found Duncan snoring in one of the recliners. The old man's eyes snapped open the minute Matt walked in.

"You never were much good at following orders," Duncan grumbled.

"I'd say that sounds suspiciously like the pot calling the kettle black."

"I'm used to giving orders," Duncan retorted defensively.

"Not around here apparently."

"Damn fool rules. All I wanted to do was make sure she was okay."

At dawn they were still growling about hospital bureaucracy when the surgeon entered the waiting room. Dr. Mitchell was with him and their expressions were somber. Matt's heart promptly thundered against his ribs.

"Grant, what is it?" Duncan asked, but Dr. Mitchell deferred to the specialist.

"We have a bit of a problem," the surgeon said. "Meg's showing signs of rejecting the kidney. At this point, it's nothing to get too excited about. We've increased the medication and we're watching her closely. The next few hours should give us some answers."

Matt started out of the room.

"Where do you think you're going?" the doctor asked.

"To see her."

"Absolutely not. I want her to remain in total isolation for the time being," he said adamantly.

Matt felt ready to explode, but Dr. Mitchell placed a restraining hand on his arm. "I know it's difficult, son, but it's better for Meg this way. You don't want to add to the risks. An infection might be the final blow."

Matt felt as though his own life were slowly seeping out of him, but he took a deep breath and nodded. "I'll be here, though, if anything changes."

"We'll find you."

When they'd gone, Duncan said, "I think I'll go call Jackie. She ought to know."

"What about your son?"

"I'll stop by his room. Are you going to be okay for a while?"

"I'll be fine," he said, but his voice lacked conviction. There was no way he'd be fine until Meg was out of danger. And if she died... He closed his eyes and tried to block out the cold emptiness that threatened to engulf him. That just couldn't happen. Not when he'd waited all his life to find her.

Images from the last few weeks flashed through his mind: Meg's head thrown back, her hair flying, as she whirled on a dance floor; her eyes lit with excitement as she skated in the moonlight; her lips curved in an amused, tolerant smile when he couldn't get the camp fire going; the stubborn tilt of her chin and flash of fire in her eyes when she was furious with him; the provocative allure of her body in outrageously sexy lingerie and fur; the vulnerability in her eyes as she awaited her parents' arrival.

The images were there and gone, as elusive as Meg had been when they'd first met. Now, though, she had confessed to loving him. She was his. He couldn't lose her. He wanted to scream and pound his fists against the walls at his inability to do anything. Matt was used to being able to fix things, to taking charge. Now he could only sit on the sidelines and wait while Meg fought alone.

Though it seemed like forever and more, it was only a short time later when Jackie Blake came in and sat down beside him. He opened his eyes and tried to manage a smile. It wouldn't come.

"You look like the very devil," she said.

"I feel like it, too."

"Why don't you go home and clean up a bit. The doctor says we're in for a long wait. You don't want to be a mess when you finally get to see Meg."

"I can't leave," he said simply. "I'm scared to death something will happen while I'm gone."

She squeezed his hand. "Waiting's the hardest part, but she's going to make it. I just know it."

"Tell me about her. Tell me what she was like when she was a little girl. I saw the picture Duncan has of her, and she looked so happy."

Jackie smiled. "She was. Oh, she was such a lovely child." Her eyes sparkled as she reminisced. "As a toddler, she was always into everything. I've never seen such curiosity. By the time she was in grade school, if I didn't keep my eye on her every minute, she'd be up in a tree or on the roof. They say boys are the ones who like to take things apart and put them back together, but Meg was like that. At one point I don't think we had a single working clock in the house."

Her smile widened. "She had so many friends, too. There'd been times I'd felt guilty that I'd only been able to have the one child, but having all of those other children around almost made up for it. I told myself that Meg probably hardly noticed that she was an only child."

A shadow of pain flitted across her face and Matt knew instantly the direction in which her thoughts had gone.

"And then she developed diabetes," he said.

"Yes. At first we had no idea what was wrong with her. She was thirsty all the time and so lethargic. For a girl who'd had so much energy, it just didn't seem right. She was only in junior high, but we actually wondered if she might be on drugs. You read all the time about how early kids start experimenting. We even confronted her about it and she just stared at us as though we were crazy. I've never seen such a look of hurt in anyone's eyes."

Matt recalled that look well and realized how hearing the same accusation from him must have compounded her pain.

"Finally we couldn't ignore the symptoms any longer and we took her to Dr. Mitchell. He diagnosed the diabetes. Jonathan and I were beside ourselves. We accused ourselves of failing her in some way, of being to blame. We tried to be supportive, but I guess we were so stunned and so worried, we overreacted. We tried to do everything for her, to make up for the friends who'd been scared away. Parents of teenage girls are protective enough as it is. We were worse. It's no wonder Meg resented us."

She gazed at Matt, her eyes filled with regret. "If only we'd done things differently."

"She said it herself. She'd probably still be here today. You couldn't have prevented this."

"Perhaps not," she replied wistfully, "But we would have had the last six years with her."

Jackie's words and their unspoken meaning hung over them during the rest of the interminable day and night. She and Duncan took turns staying with Matt, while the other visited with Jonathan who was equally frantic about Meg. It was late the following morning before the doctors finally came back with good news.

"She's stabilized," the surgeon said. "I don't want to get your hopes too high, but I'd say we're probably out of the woods for the time being. You'll have to gown up, but you can see her now. Don't stay more than a few minutes each."

Matt let Duncan and Jackie go in first. Although he told himself it was only right that they see her before he did, he knew fear was making him reluctant. He was so terribly afraid of what he would find.

When his turn finally came, his pulse raced and he drew in a deep calming breath. He didn't want Meg to sense his concern. He wanted to be as brave as she had been. It was odd how he'd been so brave as a soldier, facing his own death every day, only to be so terrified now.

He opened the door hesitantly and stepped inside, covered in a green gown and wearing a mask. Meg gave him a wobbly grin.

"Hi there," he said softly.

"Hi yourself," she whispered hoarsely. "I like your outfit."

"The very best in designer gowns. How're you feeling?"

"Like I've been to war and back with a couple of old soldiers."

"The doctor says you're going to be fine."

"I think that's a slight exaggeration. He says I'm over the first hurdle."

"The rest will be a breeze," he said with confidence he didn't feel.

Meg nodded, then drifted back to sleep, clinging to Matt's hand. Matt stood watching her for a few more minutes, his heart in his throat.

"Dear God," he prayed silently. "Let her make it. Please let her make it."

The next day when Meg awoke she felt a little stronger, and the day after that she was stronger still. She actually began to believe what the doctors and Matt had been telling her—that the worst was over. She was worried about Matt, though. His eyes were tired and he seemed on the edge of collapse.

"Matthew Flanagan, I want you to go home and get some sleep," she ordered.

"My, my," he retorted. "You are feeling better."

"At the rate you're going, I'll soon feel better than you do."

"Then we can share a room here while we both recover."

"Forget that. I'll be back at work, which is something you should consider doing."

"Are you afraid I won't be able to support you?"

"I don't need you to support me."

"Husbands support their wives. It's the natural order of things."

"It *was* the natural order of things. Today couples share responsibilities. If and when I decide to get married, I certainly have no intention of giving up my work."

"If and when?"

"No one's asked me... at least no one I was interested in marrying."

"I'm glad you brought that up because I've been thinking."

"I thought you were a man of action."

"Exactly. I've been thinking it's time we took some action."

"I know I'm all doped up here, Flanagan, but you're not making any sense."

"I was thinking we ought to be planning a wedding for the minute you get out of here. I'd suggest we do it now, but hospital green is definitely not your color."

"Oh, Matt," she whispered, her eyes shining. She wanted so badly to marry him and yet...

"I can't," she said at last.

"What do you mean you can't? Two minutes ago, you were carrying on because I hadn't asked."

"I was not carrying on."

He glowered at her.

"Okay, so maybe I was hinting a little, but it won't work. My future's too uncertain."

"A few weeks ago, you wouldn't even think about the future," he reminded her, stalking around the room, pausing occasionally to scowl at her. "You were determined to live only in the present. Now that's what I'm doing. You and I are going to have one hell of a present. We'll let the future take care of itself."

Meg blinked and scowled at him. "Stop shouting. You're not supposed to shout a proposal."

"I'll do whatever I have to do to get through to you. Don't you remember what the marriage vows say, 'In sickness and in health'?"

"But you can't want—"

"I most definitely do want," he corrected adamantly. "If you weren't lying here all bandaged up, I'd show you exactly how much I do want you."

Meg sighed, then grinned at him. "My lips aren't bandaged," she said softly.

He studied her cautiously. "Does that mean..."

"If you're foolish enough to want me after all I've put you through, I'll marry you."

Matt eased himself down on the side of the bed carefully, then bent over and touched his lips to hers. The kiss lost a little of its usual effectiveness through the mask, but a shiver still tripped down her spine.

"I love you, Margaret Blake."

"And I love you, Matthew Flanagan," she whispered and the smile that lit her face was every bit as joyous as the one with which Matt had fallen in love.

The door suddenly squeaked closed, but not before the two of them saw Duncan slip away. The old devil had a very satisfied expression on his face.

* * * * *

Take 4 Silhouette Intimate Moments novels and a surprise gift
FREE

Then preview 4 brand-new Silhouette Intimate Moments novels—delivered to your door as soon as they come off the presses! If you decide to keep them, you pay just $2.49 each*—a 9% saving off the retail price, *with no additional charges for postage and handling!*

Silhouette Intimate Moments novels are not for everyone. They were created to give you a more detailed, more exciting reading experience, filled with romantic fantasy, intense sensuality and stirring passion.

Start with 4 Silhouette Intimate Moments novels and a surprise gift absolutely FREE. They're yours to keep without obligation. You can always return a shipment and cancel at any time.

Simply fill out and return the coupon today!

* Plus 49¢ postage and handling per shipment in Canada.

Silhouette Intimate Moments®

COMING IN OCTOBER

SEA GATE
by
MAURA SEGER

Atlantis . . . land of the imagination. Or is it real?

Suppose a man of our world were to meet a woman who might not be exactly what she seemed. What if they found not only love, but a way to cross bridges that had never before been crossed?

Travel with them in SEA GATE, a very special love story about two very special people. Coming next month, only from Silhouette Intimate Moments.

Don't miss it!

IM209-1

Silhouette Desire

COMING NEXT MONTH

#379 MIDNIGHT RAMBLER—Linda Barlow
Headmistress Dany Holland had suspicions about Max Rambler.
Vampires belonged in storybooks, but when strange nocturnal events
threatened her students, she was determined to find out Max's secret.

#380 EAGLE'S PREY—Lucy Gordon
Photographing eagles had brought Sara to Farraway Island, but it
was Rorke Calvin who kept her there. His plans for revenge were
almost ripe—could she convince him to give them up for love?

#381 GIVE AND TAKE—Anna Schmidt
Set designer Marlo Fletcher was asked to dress the windows of
Carrington's department store. Sparks flew between her and
Josh Carrington—who would think that matters of the heart were
such a give-and-take business?

#382 NO LAUGHING MATTER—Marie Nicole
Writer Marti McGregor lived by her wit and spent a lot of time hiding
behind it. Producer Stephen Townsend was determined to break
through her defenses—for love was no laughing matter.

#383 CARNIVAL MADNESS—Erin Ross
Tired of nothing but parties, Elizabeth fled the latest Venetian
costume ball, only to find herself in the arms of a waiting gondolier.
Roberto was nothing that he seemed . . . but all that she desired.

#384 LOST AND FOUND—Robin Elliott
Kendra had no intention of getting involved with her neighbor *or* his
pet rabbit. But Joseph wasn't about to let this enchanting woman
misplace the love he'd searched a lifetime to find!

ATTRACTIVE, SPACE SAVING BOOK RACK

Display your most prized novels on this handsome and sturdy book rack. The hand-rubbed walnut finish will blend into your library decor with quiet elegance, providing a practical organizer for your favorite hard-or soft-covered books.

Only $9.95

Approximately 16" x 8" when assembled

Assembles in seconds!

To order, rush your name, address and zip code, along with a check or money order for $10.70* ($9.95 plus 75¢ postage and handling) payable to *Silhouette Books*.

Silhouette Books
Book Rack Offer
901 Fuhrmann Blvd.
P.O. Box 1396
Buffalo, NY 14269-1396

Offer not available in Canada.

BKR-2A

*New York and Iowa residents add appropriate sales tax.

Starting in October...

SHADOWS ON THE NILE

by

Heather Graham Pozzessere

A romantic short story in six installments from best-selling author Heather Graham Pozzessere.

The first chapter of this intriguing romance will appear in all Silhouette titles published in October. The remaining five chapters will appear, one per month, in Silhouette Intimate Moments' titles for November through March '88.

Don't miss "*Shadows on the Nile*"—a special treat, coming to you in October. Only from Silhouette Books.

Be There!